I0618989

It all started with a simple blackmail scheme.

The Travelers, con artists who specialize in stealing from criminals, find themselves short on cash and plan on making a quick $100,000 blackmailing a prosecuting attorney with a taste for call girls. Convincing a call girl to partner with them was easy, but they hadn't counted on the dogged persistence of a rule-bending FBI agent and the maliciousness of the criminals whose help they need to make their escape.

Broke and on the run, they must outmaneuver the FBI while they set up an even riskier robbery to recoup their losses. And in the meantime, a criminal gang they'd scammed previously is back on their trail, seeking revenge.

*Grifters' Hopscotch* is a fast-paced thriller that will keep you guessing. If you like criminal intrigue, ingenious suspense, and unpredictable plot twists, you'll love the tenth novel in the Travelers series.

# GRIFTERS' HOPSCOTCH

## THE TRAVELERS: BOOK TEN

## MICHAEL P. KING

BLURRED LINES PRESS

Blurred Lines Press

Grifters' Hopscotch

Michael P. King

ISBN 978-1-952711-15-2

Cover design by Paramita Bhattacharjee at creativeparamita.com

*Grifters' Hopscotch* is a work of fiction. The names, characters, places, and events are products of the author's imagination or are used fictitiously. Any similarity to real persons or places is entirely coincidental.

*Always for Sarah*

# 1

At 2:00 p.m. the Travelers, con artists going by the aliases Randy and Jodi Sutton, were sitting in a rental car in the parking lot of the Sunrise Arms Motel at the freeway interchange in Putney, Ohio. It was a hot September afternoon. They'd been tailing Blaine County Prosecuting Attorney Terry Brighton for several days, following him as he drove from home to the county administrative building to various lunchtime diners to courthouse meetings, and he'd finally led them here. Now they were waiting to see if the information they'd paid for was correct.

"Fingers crossed," Jodi said. She shifted in her seat and smoothed out the skirt of her dress. She was in her early forties but passed for late thirties. Her auburn hair was covered by a broad-brimmed hat. She looked like a movie star traveling incognito, with her dark sunglasses, perfect smile, and flawless skin.

Randy sipped his coffee and watched the door to room 204. He was almost ten years her senior. He wore a ballcap over his gray-streaked hair, and mirrored sunglasses hid his eyes. He had the muscles of a man who worked out hard and a face that was completely forgettable.

After about an hour, Brighton—dark blue suit, red tie, thinning hair, and wire-rim glasses—came out of the motel room, glanced around as if he was afraid he might be recognized, and crossed the parking lot to his red Lexus. Randy and Jodi kept waiting.

A few minutes later, a very young blonde, small breasts and slim hips, wearing a tiny party dress, came out of the room with a leather duffel slung over her shoulder.

Randy chuckled. "Well, well. She's certainly worth the wait."

"Terry Brighton is a bad, bad boy," Jodi said.

"Wonder how he's kept this secret so long?"

"Who knows?"

The blonde got into an old silver Honda with a missing hubcap. The Travelers pulled out after her.

"Well," Jodi continued, "one thing's for certain. I'm not going to be able to seduce Brighton."

"I'd have to agree," Randy said. "That girl looks like she might still be wearing braces. So we're going to have to follow her to the next rendezvous, find a way to get her out of the room for a few minutes before he arrives—or set up our video camera in a motel window after he gets there."

"Most of these no-tell motels don't have windows at the back, so we'd probably have to set up at the front of the building on a window with a gap in the curtain."

"Even if they left the curtain gapped, do you think we could set up in front without being noticed by anyone in the parking lot? Even if they were meeting after dark, the probability of being seen is way too high."

Randy got into the left turn lane two cars behind the blonde and followed her onto Oakview Boulevard.

Jodi continued. "Are you saying we need to move on?"

"We're short on cash, baby. We've got to make this work."

"If our counterfeiter on the last job hadn't been arrested, we wouldn't be in this spot."

"He was a loudmouth. We were lucky not to get swept up with him," Randy said.

"So how do we make this work?"

"It's a desperation move, but how about if we bring her into the game?"

"She's a civilian," Jodi replied.

"She's an escort. She's already in the game—just not our game."

"What are you planning to do with her?"

"You jealous?"

"Maybe."

"It's a one-off, honey. She already knows seduction, so we won't be training her. It's just about getting her cooperation. If she's in, this job is a sure thing."

"Three-way split?"

"Yeah. We'll still make enough to set up another job."

"But if she says no?"

"That's the downside. If she says no, we've blown up the job. But it's worth the gamble. We can't do it without her. There's no time to find someone else if we want to get this done before the election, while we have the most leverage on Brighton."

"Okay, I agree. It's worth the gamble. But let's look her over first."

"Absolutely."

They followed her past the Putney State University football stadium and into a neighborhood of rundown rentals with lawn chairs, pizza boxes, and beer cans scattered across the front lawns. She pulled up the driveway of a white clapboard house with peeling paint and rickety wooden steps, parked behind a black Jeep, and went inside.

Randy and Jodi pulled to the curb at the end of the block.

"This is a party neighborhood," Randy said.

"She's probably a student working her way through college."

"That's the stereotype, isn't it?"

Twenty minutes later, the blonde came out of the house wearing an unzipped sweatshirt over leggings and a sports bra, a gym bag over her shoulder. Randy and Jodi got out of their car and followed her onto campus to the student recreational center, where she went inside. Randy and Jodi sat down on a bench near the bus stop.

"She looks older without makeup. She's making herself up younger for her job," Jodi said.

"To a middle-age guy like Brighton, she looks like a kid. That's all that matters."

A class period ended. Students crowded the sidewalks and the bike lanes, some headed for their next class, others headed home. The campus circulator bus stopped at the bus stop. A few students got off carrying gym bags and crossed the street to the rec center. Randy and Jodi kept waiting. A little over an hour later, the blonde came out of the rec center, red-faced and sweaty.

"You ready to try her?" Randy asked.

"Let's do it."

They crossed the street and started after her, catching up at the first intersection on the way back to her house.

"Excuse me," Jodi said. "Can we talk with you a minute?"

The blonde looked them up and down. "Do I know you?"

"Not yet," Randy said. "But we have a job offer we think you'll be interested in."

"We know you're with the escort agency," Jodi added.

"If you want to book me, you have to go through the agency. And I don't do couples."

"We're not interested in booking you," Randy said. "We're interested in making you an offer that will net you about thirty thousand dollars."

"Thirty thousand dollars? Impossible."

"But it's not," Jodi said.

"Then it's crazy dangerous. Nothing safe nets thirty thousand dollars. What exactly do you expect me to do?"

Jodi continued. "Just what you've been doing."

"Going with a man?"

"That's all."

"That doesn't make sense."

"It will after we explain it."

"Look, I need to go home and shower."

"Then let's walk back to your place."

"You know where I live?"

"We're parked on the street down the block from your house."

"We followed you from your last date," Randy added.

"With Terry?"

Jodi nodded.

"You're creeping me out."

"If we wanted to hurt you," Jodi said, "we'd have done it by now."

The blonde thought for a moment, shrugged, and started walking. "I guess that's right."

Jodi fell in beside her, Randy walking just behind.

"So," Jodi said, "the old guy, Terry. Do you know who he is?"

She shook her head. "I know he's safe and easy to please."

"He's Terry Brighton. Do you know what he does?"

"No idea."

"He's the prosecuting attorney."

"For this county?"

"Yes."

"Wow. Let me get this straight. Terry—the guy I've been meeting a couple of times a week for six months—is the prosecutor for the county?"

"Yep."

"You sure it's him?"

"We've been following him. That's how we found you."

"This is crazy."

"If you say so."

"So does the thirty thousand have something to do with him?"

Jodi nodded. "He's up for reelection. We want to make a video of him with you."

"You're going to blackmail him?"

"We're going to blackmail him."

"I don't want anyone to take a video of me. I'm not a porn actor. There're no images of me on the internet, and it's going to stay that way."

They stopped on the sidewalk in front of her house. "No one's going to do anything with the video," Jodi said. "Think about it.

Brighton won't want the video posted. It would ruin his career. That's why he'll pay. We don't want the video posted because we don't want any evidence that we scammed Brighton. We're going to use the video as leverage to get paid and then we're going to destroy it."

"What if he thinks I'm involved?"

"You cry. Blame him. Claim the video will ruin your future."

"Which it would," she said.

"All the more reason why it won't get out. You're part of our team, and we'll make sure it's destroyed."

"We're going to walk you through the job," Randy said. "Hold your hand all the way. You'll make thirty grand."

"Does the escort service know what you're up to?"

"No. This will be just the three of us."

"And Terry."

"That's everyone."

"How do I know you just won't cheat me after you get the money?"

"Because that's not how we work," Randy said. "Cheating your partners is bad for business. You work with us, we get paid, you get paid."

"Can I think about it?"

"Tomorrow. Give us a call before noon." Randy handed her a card with a phone number on one side. He and Jodi walked away.

CHRISSIE MAKAROVA STOOD on her stoop and watched the couple walk down to a car parked at the end of the block before she unlocked the door and went into her house.

"Hey," she called out. No one answered. Bruce and Melanie must have still been on campus. She dropped her gym bag on the floor of her bedroom and took her fluffy robe with her into the bathroom across the hall. She locked the door, turned on the water in the shower to let it get hot, and peeled off her sweaty clothes.

Thirty thousand dollars. She made decent money as an escort—enough to pay her bills and save a little cash—but ever since her mom's early onset dementia had put her in the care center, she'd been slowly running through her savings. Had to take out an extra student loan this semester. Thirty thousand would be a big help.

She got into the shower and let the water spray down on her head. She'd already had sex with Terry, so nothing new there. What were the possible downsides? The escort service could find out about the scam and fire her. She'd lose her easy job. But she was a valuable employee, so they wouldn't fire her without proof. And how would they get that if Terry kept his mouth shut? So not much risk there. What else? The blackmailers could cheat her out of her share, and she'd have helped them for nothing. But that didn't seem likely. And her situation wouldn't be any worse than it was now. Terry could go to the police. She could be arrested, thrown in jail. But then he'd lose the election, so that wasn't going to happen. She stepped forward to let the water spray on her back while she soaped her front.

Easy money. Almost too easy. She finished washing, got out of the shower, and toweled off. There were risks, but they didn't seem that significant. Her mom's social security covered most of her care, but not the extras that Chrissie wanted for her. The single room and the cognitive skills specialist, those were out of pocket. Thirty thousand dollars would go a long way. But if she made the video, the black-mailers would see her having sex with Terry, which was—she had to admit—creepy. She toweled her hair. Of course, they wouldn't be in the room. It would be like it was a film, and she didn't know them, so it wouldn't be as creepy as someone she knew watching her or seeing a tape of her. Thirty thousand dollars. She pulled on her fluffy robe and started toward her bedroom. The TV was on in the living room. She peeked in. Bruce was sprawled across the sofa, eating potato chips out of the bag and watching a sports round-up show.

"Hey, Chrissie."

"Hey."

"You done in the bathroom?"

"Yes. What are you doing about dinner?"

"Don't know."

"When's Melanie get back?"

"Not until late. She'll eat at work." He turned back to the TV.

Chrissie went down the hall to her room. Thirty thousand dollars was a lot of money. Money she needed. The tape would never get out. Even with the creep factor, she couldn't turn the money down.

RANDY AND JODI sat in a booth in an Italian restaurant, drinking red wine and waiting for their orders. It was still a little early—6:15 p.m.—but the room was mostly full, and the background banter and the light jazz on the overhead speakers made private conversation possible.

"Do you think she'll bite?" Jodi asked.

"What do you think?"

"I think she'll talk herself into it."

"I think you're right." Randy sipped his wine. "You played it just right, sherpa-ing the play so she'd feel like you had her back."

"Thank you. You were very managerial."

"That's why we're such a great team."

"But if she says no?"

"Can't make the video without her. We haven't really spent any money yet. We'll just have to suck up our losses and move on."

"See if any of our contacts know about another quick job?"

"And hope our money holds out."

THE NEXT DAY, midafternoon, Randy and Jodi walked through from the bowling alley to the bar of Anytime Bowling, an old-fashioned bowling alley on the outskirts of town. A grizzled bartender wearing black suspenders stood behind the bar, washing glasses. The young blonde, wearing leggings with an oversize sweater, sat at a Formica-topped table near the far wall. All the other tables were empty. Jodi sat down cattycorner to the blonde and Randy sat across from her.

"Interesting choice for the meet," Randy said.

"I've never been here before," the blonde replied.

"Beer?" Jodi asked.

She nodded.

Jodi went up to the bar and came back with three tap beers.

"Thanks," the blonde said. She sipped her beer and looked from Jodi to Randy.

"Might as well start with introductions," Randy said. "I'm Randy Sutton and this is my wife, Jodi."

"I'm Chrissie Makarova."

"We're glad you decided to work with us," Jodi said.

"So this is what you do?"

"This isn't the first time, if that's what you're asking."

"It's very simple," Randy continued. "You tell us about your next appointment with Brighton. We arrive at the motel room and set up the camera."

"How big is it?"

"Tiny. You'll forget it's there, and you'll see me place it. Brighton will come. You'll do your thing. He'll leave. We'll come get the camera."

"That's all?"

"We deal with the rest of it," Jodi said.

"When will I get my money?"

"We'll contact Brighton. He'll have to get the money together, so a few days. Less than a week for sure."

Chrissie nodded and sipped her beer.

"All that's the easy part," Randy said.

"Then what's the hard part?"

"When he tells you about the blackmail."

Jodi continued. "You have to act surprised, confused, afraid."

"Can you be convincing?" Randy added.

"I can be convincing."

"Are you sure? Once we start, there's no backing out."

"He's a regular. Twice a week I convince him I enjoy having sex with him."

Randy studied her face. "This is a little different from that."

"I know. I can do it."

"Okay, then. When do you see him next?"

"The day after tomorrow. Unless he changes up because he has a commitment."

"We'll be expecting your call."

Randy and Jodi walked out of the bowling alley into the hot bright afternoon.

"Almost too easy," Randy replied.

"She doesn't know what she's getting into."

"She's just thinking about the money."

"She might fold up," Jodi said.

"Still worth the risk. We'll just have to keep an eye on her."

# 2

Two days later, shortly after 1:00 p.m., Randy and Jodi met Chrissie at the Buena Vista Motel out by the industrial park. She was wearing a tiny party dress, and her hair was braided as if she was fourteen. The room held a king-size bed, a small table with two chairs, and a flat-screen TV. The window curtain was closed. Randy attached a tiny camera to the top of the curtain with a bit of double-sided tape.

"Is that all?" Chrissie asked.

"That's it. Contains a Bluetooth transmitter. We'll capture the recording on a computer in the parking lot."

Jodi took Chrissie by the shoulders. "You can do this. You're in control. This is your space. Forget about the camera, and just be yourself."

"I know," she replied. "I'll get it done."

"Thirty thousand dollars."

"Thirty thousand dollars."

Randy and Jodi crossed the parking lot to their car, opened a laptop computer, and checked to make sure the camera was functioning.

"Picture's a little grainy," Randy said, "but the camera captures most of the room."

"The image is good enough," Jodi replied.

Brighton's Lexus pulled into the parking lot.

"There he is," Jodi said. They slid down in their seats as Brighton walked across the parking lot carrying a shopping bag. They sat back up after he went inside the room. On the camera, they could see him kissing Chrissie. Then he handed her the shopping bag. She disappeared into the bathroom. He shrugged out of his suitcoat and kicked off his shoes. When Chrissie came out of the bathroom, she was wearing a white schoolgirl shirt tied to show her belly and a short plaid skirt that revealed a pair of white granny panties. Brighton came around the bed to meet her.

"If every job were only this easy," Randy said.

Brighton stripped off his clothes and pushed Chrissie back onto the bed. The camera had a front shot of his face. "There's no way he can lie his way out of that," Jodi said.

"No need to watch anymore, but let's keep recording, just in case."

They waited until Brighton had driven off and Chrissie opened the door and waved at them before they crossed over to the motel room. Chrissie was back in her party dress, her hair now in a ponytail. "Did you get what you needed?"

"Yes," Jodi replied. "You did a great job. We got a great shot of your back and his front. Do you want to see it?"

"No. I don't want to know what I look like when I'm with him. It's embarrassing."

Jodi rubbed her back. "I understand. Don't worry. No one's going to see it except Brighton, and trust me, he's not going to be turned on."

Randy unstuck the camera from the top edge of the curtain. He turned to Chrissie. "You okay? We could go have a drink and talk about it if you want to."

"I'm okay."

"Just think about the money."

"When does Terry get the video?"

"Tomorrow. No reason to waste any time."

THE NEXT DAY AFTER LUNCH, when Terry Brighton got back to his office at the county administrative building, he found a small, padded envelope sitting on his desk. Inside was a cell phone, a thumb drive, and a handwritten note:

*From the motel yesterday. Have a look at the movie. It will cost you $100,000 for the original. Put the money together. We'll call later with the where and when.*

Brighton got up and shut the door to his office. Then he plugged the thumb drive into his personal iPad and clicked on the file. His back was to the camera. Chrissie was wearing the schoolgirl outfit he'd brought her yesterday. As he took her to the bed the camera filmed his face straight on. There was no deniability. If this video got out, he'd lose the election for sure. He stopped the video and pulled the thumb drive. Then he looked at the phone. It was a cheap, prepaid one you bought from a convenience store. There were no numbers in the address book.

He sighed. He wasn't married, but that didn't matter. Chrissie looked way too young. And even if she was twenty-one, he'd dressed her up to play a teenager, which made him look like a pervert. He'd been careless. Dug this hole all by himself. He could skim the $100,000 from his election war chest, pay the price for being an idiot, but would that be the end of it? Would the blackmailers actually delete the original file, or would they just ask for more money later?

He needed to find these people and deal with them, and he needed to do it discreetly. He certainly couldn't let his campaign manager find out. He needed help—someone out of his chain of command who could be trusted. Someone who owed him a favor. Not the sheriff or anyone in his office. He swiveled his chair to look out the window. Smitty. He'd know what to do. Brighton got out his personal smartphone. "Smitty? I need to see you. I've got a problem I need your help with."

When Brighton pulled into the main parking lot of Memorial

Park, he saw FBI agent Joe Smith's black Ford Explorer parked at the far end of the lot. After he parked beside the Explorer, Agent Smith, a burly man with a blond crewcut, climbed out of it and got in the passenger's seat of the Lexus.

"What's up, Terry? Sounded urgent on the phone."

"Well, Smitty, I've stepped in some dog shit, and I need your help." He explained the situation.

Smith shook his head. "Call girls during the election cycle?"

"I know."

"Who knew where you were meeting?"

"No one."

"Someone did. And they knew ahead of time. Unless the call girl set the camera herself."

"She wouldn't do that."

"The obvious answer is often the right one."

"She's a college student."

"Aren't they all? Did you vet her?"

Brighton nodded.

"What's her name and address?"

Brighton told him and Smith wrote them down.

"Okay, I'm going to look into this girl. Can you get the money?"

"Yes."

"Then get it ready. You might have to pay them. If the black-mailers contact you, try to stall them, and then call me."


MEANWHILE, Randy, Jodi, and Chrissie were sitting around a table in the back corner of a Caffeination coffee shop. The lunch rush was over, and the only other customers were seated at the front windows.

"Brighton should have opened the envelope by now," Randy said.

"So he's going to start pointing fingers," Jodi added. "If he accuses you, remember, you should be focused on you and how the video affects your reputation and your future."

Chrissie nodded. "My future will be destroyed."

"Exactly."

"We'll let him stew overnight. Let the paranoia build. Then we'll set up the rendezvous," Randy said.

"I want to be there when you pick up the money," Chrissie said.

"That's the riskiest part of the plan," Jodi said. "You sure you want to do that?"

"No offense, guys, but once the money's in play, I'm staying with you until I get my share."

"It's your call," Randy said.

AGENT SMITH WENT BACK to the FBI field office downtown, got on his desktop computer, and went into the FBI database to find out everything he could about Chrissie Makarova. She was a US citizen. Her father was unknown. Her mother was a naturalized citizen from Ukraine. She was, in fact, a college student. She had no arrest record, not even a speeding ticket. He called Brighton. "The girl is squeaky clean."

"What did I tell you?"

"Doesn't mean she isn't guilty this time."

"I'm going to meet her."

"You sure you should do that?"

"We need to push her, see if you're right. If she's involved, we could use her to find the others."

"Okay, you push her. Just let me know where you're going to meet."

BRIGHTON ENDED the call with Smith and found Chrissie's phone number in his address book under *Plumber*. There was a knock on his office door. Sherry, his administrative assistant, stuck her head in. "I've got the files you wanted."

"Thanks, Sherry. Just put them on the credenza."

She carried in a thick stack of files and set them on the side table by the door.

After she closed the door, Brighton input Chrissie's phone number. It went to voice mail. "We need to meet."

He ended the call and picked up the files from the credenza. As he was starting to look through the top one, his smartphone rang.

"Yes?"

"Sugar, you're booked for tomorrow."

"It's not like that. Someplace public where we won't be recognized."

"What's this about?"

"I'm not talking on the phone."

"You're scaring me."

"You ought to be scared. We need to meet as soon as possible."

"How about the stadium parking lot? There's nothing going on there today."

"Can you meet now?"

"I'll be at the north end of the lot on the west side of the stadium in twenty minutes."

Brighton ended the call and speed-dialed Smith to tell him about the meeting. Then he pulled on his suit coat and left his office.

Sherry looked up from her desktop computer as he came through the outer office. "I'll be back in an hour," he said.

Brighton drove into the Putney State University stadium parking lot and rolled up toward the north end of lot, passing random parked cars until he spotted Chrissie's old Honda. He pulled in beside her and waved for her to come over to his car. She slid into the passenger's seat. She was wearing jeans and a sweatshirt.

"What's so urgent?"

"Chrissie, someone made a video of our meeting yesterday."

"What? Impossible. Is this your idea of a joke?"

"I'm not kidding. I'm being blackmailed. Has anyone gotten in touch with you?"

"No one. Is this video from inside the motel room?"

"Yes."

"Jesus. The whole time?"

"I didn't look at the whole thing. Just enough to know it's real."

"My God. What are you going to do? If that video goes out on social media, I'm ruined." Chrissie started crying. "My friends, my mom—no one knows. I'll never be able to get a real job."

"*You'll* be ruined? What about me?"

She wiped her eyes on the sleeve of her sweatshirt. "Are you going to pay them?"

"I have to," Brighton replied.

"God, God, God. What a mess. We shouldn't see each other for a while."

"You think?"

"Let me know when this is all over with." She got out of Brighton's car.

CHRISSIE WAITED for him to drive away before she called Jodi. "Just spoke to Terry."

"Not on the phone. Let's meet at the last place."

Randy and Jodi were sitting at an umbrella table outside the Caffeination coffee shop when Chrissie arrived. "What did he say?" Randy asked.

"He told me about the video."

"Did he accuse you of being involved?"

"No, he asked me if I'd been contacted."

"So he thinks you're in the clear, or he was testing you."

"Testing me?"

"He's a prosecuting attorney. He probably thinks he's good at spotting lies."

"So what do I do now?"

"Nothing. We'll get the ball rolling tomorrow. You shouldn't meet with him anymore."

"I'm not going to."

"Good. We'll keep you up to speed."

. . .

AGENT SMITH, sitting in his Explorer down the street from the Caffeination coffee shop, focused his camera on Chrissie's friends and took several pictures with a telephoto lens. A middle-age man and a slightly younger woman. Dressed to fit in. The man unremarkable, the woman a knock-out. Who the hell were they?

Smith watched them through the camera. Chrissie got up and walked back to her car. Her friends got into a gray Cadillac Escalade, Ohio plates. He snapped a picture. He wasn't going to be able to tail them in his Explorer. If they were players, they'd spot him, and he wasn't ready to tip his hand. The best thing to do was run their pictures and the license plate through the database.

On his way back to the FBI field office, he called Brighton.

"Anything?" Brighton asked.

"She went straight from you to a meeting with a couple at a Caffeination coffee shop."

"So you were right."

"Maybe. I'll know more after I run some checks."

Smith scanned the photos of the couple into his computer and ran the photos through the FBI's and Interpol's databases. Nothing. The license plate led to a car registration in the name of Randy Sutton, but there was no corresponding driver's license. He tapped into the US Marshals' witness protection database. Nothing. Either the couple were deep undercover government agents, or they were serious criminals. It was time to interview Chrissie Makarova.

Smith drove out to the Putney State University campus and parked on the street in front of Chrissie's house. Her car was in the driveway, as well as a black jeep registered to Bruce Gibbons. Smith walked up to the front door and knocked. No one answered. He knocked again. No one. He went back to his SUV and waited.

About half an hour later, he saw Chrissie coming down the sidewalk from the direction of campus. She was still wearing the jeans and sweatshirt she'd been wearing at the coffee shop. A bookbag was slung over her shoulder. He got out of his SUV and met her on the sidewalk in front of her house. "Ms. Makarova?"

She looked at him blankly.

He showed his FBI ID.

"What's this about?"

"Could you get in my SUV, please?"

"I don't know if I want to do that."

"Ms. Makarova, please cooperate. I'm helping Terry Brighton."

Chrissie climbed into the passenger's seat and put her bookbag on the floor between her legs. Smith got behind the wheel. She looked at him expectantly.

"Who was the couple you met with at the Caffeination coffee shop on West Elm?"

"I don't know what you're talking about."

He passed her a photo. "That's you and that's the couple I'm talking about."

"You were following me?"

"I told you that I'm helping Mr. Brighton. The two of you were together. A video was made. I expect your cooperation. Who's that couple?"

"I don't know. They were asking directions."

"Directions?"

"They're visiting their son. Wanted to avoid the traffic near campus."

"You can do better than that. Those two people aren't alumni or parents of a student. Who are they and how you know them?"

"You're talking crazy."

"You think I'm talking crazy? You're in over your head. Trying to blackmail Mr. Brighton—did you really think you could get away with it? Tell me who those people are."

"I don't know." Chrissie reached for the doorhandle, but Smith locked the SUV passenger's door before she could open it. "You can't keep me here."

"You want to go to jail for prostitution? For conspiracy to commit blackmail? How do you think your life will turn out then?"

"I don't have anything to do with any blackmail. I've got as much to lose as Terry."

"You're so naïve. You think for a minute that your partners

wouldn't turn on you if the shoe was on the other foot? I don't care about arresting you, Ms. Makarova. Mr. Brighton doesn't care about punishing you. But I'm putting an end to this blackmail. So you're going to give up your partners, and go back to your life. Who are these people?"

She looked in her lap. If the FBI knew about the blackmail, it was all over. There'd be no $30,000. She didn't owe the Suttons anything. She'd been willing to back them on a sure thing, but she wasn't willing to put her life and her livelihood at risk to protect them. She had her own problems. How could she spin this? "Randy and Jodi Sutton. That's what they told me. They're professional crooks, I think."

"How did you meet them?"

"They came to me after I met with Terry last week. They'd been watching the motel."

"And you agreed to help them?"

"Yes. I was afraid they'd hurt me if I didn't help them. I know it was stupid. I know I shouldn't have, but since I was already breaking the law, I didn't think I had anyone to turn to."

"Well, if you want out of this jam, you're going to have to help us."

"If I help you, you'll let me go?"

"You help me, and you don't tell anyone about your relationship with Mr. Brighton. That's the deal."

"Believe me, I don't want anyone to know about my escort work. But I'm not sure how I can help you. The Suttons are calling the shots."

"Let me worry about that."

"They can't know I'm talking to you."

"They won't." He unlocked the passenger's door. "Don't do anything stupid. I'll be in touch."

Smith watched Chrissie walk up to her front door, head down, bookbag in one hand. He called Brighton.

"Smitty. What's up?"

"The girl was involved. I've interviewed her and gotten her cooperation."

"So you know who the blackmailers are?"

"Their names and their pictures don't come up on any database."

"Impossible."

"I know. Doesn't matter, though. Have you got the money?"

"I'll have it in the morning."

"Good. We're going to set a trap."

"I don't want anyone else to find out about the blackmail."

"I can't guarantee that other people won't find out about the blackmail attempt, but I can guarantee no one will find out why."

"You certain of that?"

"Yes."

"Okay then. Get them off my back."

"When they call, set up a time and place to exchange the money for the original video. We'll use Makarova to get out ahead of them."

# 3

———

The next morning, while Brighton was driving to work, the burner phone buzzed. He pulled over into a Stop & Go convenience store parking lot and read the text message.

*Have you got the money?*

He replied: *Yes.*

*You know the shuttered Kmart out by the south interchange?*

*Yes.*

*You meet us in the parking lot at eleven. You come alone in your Lexus. You put the $100,000 in a bookbag.*

*How will I know you?*

*We'll know you.*

He called Smith on his smartphone and filled him in.

"You do what you've been told. No gun. No funny business. If things go wrong, I don't want you shot."

"What are you going to do?"

"Put some people in place to make sure the blackmailers can't escape."

"You sure that's going to work?"

"Trust me. We'll have these people in custody at 11:15."

. . .

AGENT SMITH ENDED the call with Brighton and called Chrissie Makarova. "Ms. Makarova, what have you got for me?"

She told him the same thing that Brighton had told him.

"Have they checked out the area?"

"Yes."

"When will they arrive?"

"We'll be across the access road, watching from the Olive Garden, at ten-thirty."

"Driving what?"

"I won't know until they pick me up."

Smith ended the call, put his cell phone in his pocket, picked up the landline of his desk, and called the sheriff's department.

"This is Agent Smith. Could you put me through to the sheriff?"

"One moment."

"Smitty. What can I do for you?"

"I need to use your SWAT team. I've got the money exchange on a blackmail happening at eleven a.m."

"This is mighty short notice."

"I apologize. I was caught off guard myself. You'll still make the papers for being there at the takedown."

"What do you need?"

"Three cars to block exits at the old Kmart parking lot and a sniper."

"Okay, then. Meet me at the loading bay at the new jail. I'll have the SWAT team there and you can go over the op."

"On my way."


AT 10:30 A.M., Randy, Jodi, and Chrissie, all wearing throwaway gloves, sat in a stolen Ford Bronco among the employee cars at the Olive Garden across the access road from the potholed Kmart parking lot. Thick clouds scudded across the sky. The parking lot was empty, except for a small construction trailer sitting at the far end of the lot near the boarded-up building. All the entrances and exits to the access road and side streets were open.

"Chrissie," Randy said, "You ever have to deal with a belligerent client?"

"Yes."

"Emotionally, this is sort of like that. Guy feels tricked, he wants what he can't have, so we have to manage him."

"Not that you'll be doing that," Jodi said. "We stay in the car, ready to run. Randy's just getting you prepared if things turn physical."

"There he is," Randy said.

Brighton's Lexus turned into the Kmart parking lot from the north entrance, drove diagonally across the parking lot to the middle and stopped.

"Put on your masks."

They pulled ski masks down over their faces. Then Jodi drove across the access road and into the Kmart parking lot, where she circled around to about twenty feet from the Lexus. She honked her horn. Brighton, a Kevlar vest over his suitcoat, climbed out of the Lexus with a bookbag.

Randy got out of the Bronco with a tablet computer. He motioned to Brighton. "Walk forward," he said.

Brighton started walking toward the Bronco. Randy met him about halfway between the vehicles. He glanced at the construction trailer and the front of the Kmart. There was no one visible. "Hand me the bag."

Brighton pushed the bookbag into his arms. "Is the tablet for me?"

"Don't be in such a hurry." Randy unzipped the bag and looked inside. Bundles of one-hundred-dollar bills. "I'm glad you know how to follow directions." He held out the tablet to Brighton. "The password is your last name."

Brighton snatched the tablet from Randy's hands, spun on his heels, and ran back to his car.

As Randy started to jog back to the Bronco, a shot rang out, cutting into the asphalt in front of the Bronco. He glanced toward the Kmart. The next shot took out the left front tire. Randy spotted a sniper on the Kmart roof. Brighton was already speeding across the parking lot toward the building. Police sirens screamed in the distance. Jodi and Chrissie jumped out of the Bronco. Randy rushed toward them. A shot cut into the asphalt in front of him. "Run," he yelled.

As Jodi and Chrissie zigzagged back across the access road, two shots thudded into the asphalt behind them. "Jesus!" Chrissie said. "What are we going to do?"

Jodi spoke over her shoulder. "Backup car. Follow me."

They ran through the Olive Garden parking lot to a MacDonald's next door, where Randy had left a Toyota RAV4 parked on a side street. Jodi opened the driver's door. "Pull off your mask."

They pulled off their masks and got into the RAV4. "What about Randy?" Chrissie asked.

"He'll make his own way."

BRIGHTON PULLED up to the front of the Kmart and turned off his car. He sat there, his heart pounding, and tried to slow his breathing. He hadn't realized how hard dealing with the blackmailers was going to be. He glanced out his window. Smitty was walking toward him. He picked up the tablet from the passenger's seat and input the password. The only document on the machine was the motel video. He deleted it and then smacked the tablet against the steering wheel.

Smith opened the driver's door. "What the fuck are you doing, Terry? That's evidence."

Brighton kept smacking the tablet until the screen smashed and the frame bent. "Not anymore. I'm in the clear now. The crime is proven by the exchange of money. No one needs to find out why I was being blackmailed."

"You think that's the only copy?"

"I've got to take that chance."

MEANWHILE, Randy was crouched down behind the Bronco. When he jumped up to run for the access road and freedom, sniper fire pinned him down. He peeked around the left side of the bumper. A sheriff's SWAT truck was speeding across the Kmart parking lot toward him. *They wouldn't shoot an unarmed man running away in broad daylight, would they?* He clutched the bookbag to his chest, sprang up from behind the Bronco, and ran full out for the access road, swerving to the right and left as the shots peppered in around him.

When he reached the other side of the access road, the sniper fire stopped. He looked over his shoulder. The SWAT truck was closing in. He pulled off his face mask, ran through the Olive Garden parking lot, and dodged traffic as he rushed across the boulevard. He glanced over his shoulder. It would take the SWAT truck a few minutes to get through the intersection at the traffic lights. He jogged through the cars in the Best Buy parking lot, looking for an older vehicle. Something without the new computer lockouts. In the employee part of the lot, he spotted an old Dodge Dart. He could hotwire that car in his sleep. He slipped the bookbag of money onto his shoulder, picked the door lock on the Dodge, tossed the bag into the passenger's seat, and climbed in. The Dodge had half a tank of gas.

He bounced over the curb from the Best Buy parking lot into the strip mall parking lot next door and took a right turn onto the boulevard. The SWAT truck drove by him on the other side of the boulevard. He eased along, just a few miles per hour over the speed limit, moving through traffic, keeping an eye on his rearview mirror. At the next intersection, he'd make a left turn into a neighborhood of apartment buildings and disappear.

The SWAT truck's siren squealed. Randy glanced in his rearview mirror and saw the truck jump the median on the boulevard and make a U-turn to start after him, blue and red lights pulsing. Randy stomped on the gas, careened through the traffic to the intersection, and slid through the left turn, the car fishtailing as he straightened it out. He took a right at the second intersection and a left three blocks farther down. He couldn't hear the sirens anymore, so he slowed down.

Fucking Brighton. He wondered if he'd gotten to Chrissie somehow. Well, too bad. They had the money. As soon as he rendezvoused with Jodi, they'd be on the road.

He pulled over in front of a duplex to look at a map app on his smartphone. As he dug into his pants pocket for the phone, a sheriff's cruiser slid sideways in front of him, blocking the street. He put the Dodge in reverse. Another cruiser slid sideways behind him. Then the SWAT truck squealed up beside him. The voice over the loud-speaker said, "Put your hands out your window."

Randy held his hands up and slowly reached over, lowered the driver's side window, and put his hands out.

"With one hand, open the door from the outside."

He reached down and opened the door.

"Step out with your hands up. Walk backward to the back of the vehicle and kneel."

He followed the commands. Two deputies came up behind him, pushed him face down on the pavement, and cuffed him behind his back.

"How did you find me?"

The deputy on his right laughed and pointed up. "Drone. You never had a chance."

They hustled Randy toward the SWAT truck.

Another deputy opened the Dodge's passenger door, picked up the bookbag, looked inside, and tapped his comms. "We've got the money."

JODI AND CHRISSIE, Jodi behind the wheel, drove to the next intersection and turned right into a neighborhood of two-car-garage ranch houses. "Get out your phone and open your map app."

"Okay," Chrissie replied.

"Input your address."

She input the address. "Okay, in three blocks, take a right." She looked up at Jodi. "Why are we going to my place?"

Jodi made the right turn. "Does Brighton have your phone number?"

"On this phone? No. This phone is completely personal." She glanced down at the screen on her phone. "Another right at the traffic lights."

"Gotcha."

"So why are we going to my house?"

"The police don't have your face or your fingerprints. So you go home. Wait for Brighton to call your business phone. Act appropriate to whatever he tells you. Then you end it with him so that you can't get caught up in a lie in the future."

"But what if Randy's been caught?"

"He won't get caught."

"But is he does?"

"He won't say anything."

"What about my money?"

"We'll be in touch."

They didn't talk anymore, except for Chrissie calling out directions until they were near the college campus. Jodi pulled up in front of Chrissie's house.

"Play it cool," Jodi said, "and you'll stay in the clear. As soon as I hear from Randy, I'll give you a call."

Jodi drove to the nearest campus parking lot, pulled into an open space, and wiped down the front seats, doors, steering wheel and dashboard, even though she'd been wearing gloves. Then she walked away from the SUV, walked over two blocks to a corner at the edge of campus, and called a rideshare using a fake account. Campus police would be calling a towing company to collect the RAV4 within a few hours, which should hide it in the towing company's lot for a couple of days.

Class change was over with when her rideshare arrived, the sidewalk and bike lane free of students. She got into the car.

"Are you Carol?" the driver asked.

"Yes."

They pulled into traffic. Jodi looked out the window. Did Randy escape? They hadn't thought that Brighton would involve SWAT. How did he plan to keep his indiscretion a secret? Not her problem.

Right now, she had to sit tight, wait for Randy to make contact. Good thing they'd set up the safehouse.

MEANWHILE, Randy sat in the back seat of the SWAT truck, his wrists cuffed behind his back. The deputy in the front seat was in a celebratory mood, whistling as he drove out of town to the new jail facility, located at a county road intersection surrounded by farm fields.

Once they reached the jail, the deputy drove through the gate in the razor-wire-topped chain-link fence and pulled to a halt in front of a set of steel doors. Two beefy corrections officers, one with slicked-back hair, the other with a shaved head and a tightly trimmed beard, came out and led Randy up the sidewalk into booking. They uncuffed him, patted him down, emptied his pockets into a plastic bag, and entered his photo and his fingerprints into the electronic database. No one came up.

"What is your name?" the corrections officer with the slicked back hair asked.

"Lawyer."

The other officer, the one with the shaved head, looked in Randy's wallet. "The driver's license says Randy Sutton."

The first officer entered that name in the database. Randy glanced at the door to the hall. Nowhere to run. At least he knew now that his fingerprints hadn't been in the national database before. And now they'd always be associated with the Randy Sutton alias.

They took him into an interrogation room, sat him down in the plastic chair, and cuffed one wrist to the steel loop on a table that was bolted to the concrete floor. A few minutes later, a heavyset man with a blond crewcut came into the room.

The man took a toothpick out of his mouth. "I'm FBI Agent Smith."

"Lawyer."

The agent sat in the chair on the other side of the table. "We don't have to be confrontational."

"Lawyer."

"No one was hurt. You weren't carrying a gun. You could make a good deal."

"Lawyer."

"You're just going to make things worse for yourself."

"Lawyer."

"Have you got a lawyer in mind?"

"Let me make a phone call."

Smith uncuffed him and led him to a wall phone out in the hall. Randy dialed a phone number that he'd memorized. "Baby?"

"Where are you?" Jodi replied.

"In jail. I need a lawyer."

"I'm on it."

JODI SET the burner phone on the coffee table and looked in her smartphone to find the phone number of Betty Ricardo, a lawyer with a reputation for sharp elbows. Jodi called her personal number. "Ms. Ricardo? Jodi Sutton."

"How did you get this number?"

"I was told that you were the person to hire for criminal work if money were no object."

"I'm listening."

"I'd like for you to represent my husband."

"What's he charged with?"

"Hasn't been arraigned yet. Probably something to do with black-mail or extortion."

"Where is he?"

"County jail."

"I'll need a fifteen thousand dollar retainer. I bill two hundred an hour. If I need to bring in extra counsel, detectives, or other experts, those costs are additional."

"Do you accept cash?"

"Yes. I'll write you a receipt."

"Where do you want to meet to accept the retainer?"

"Come to my office."

"I'll be there in thirty minutes."

Jodi ended the call. She walked through to the kitchen and filled a glass with water from the tap. Fifteen thousand dollars. That would leave them with $17,000. What a clusterfuck. Well, it didn't matter. She was going to spend every penny if that's what it took to break Randy out of jail.

AN HOUR AND A HALF LATER, a middle-aged woman in a rumpled skirt suit hustled into the interrogation room. "Mr. Sutton? I'm Betty Ricardo, your wife hired me to represent you."

"Pleased to meet you. Are we speaking confidentially?"

"Yes."

"No one can hear or see us?"

"Someone could look through the window in the door, but that's all."

"What am I being charged with?"

"Extortion. But we'll find out the details at the arraignment."

"How is this a federal case?"

"What do you mean?"

"The only cop I've seen in here is FBI."

"I haven't seen any paperwork yet. Do you want to tell me what happened so that I can begin to work on your defense?"

He shook his head. "I want the proceedings to go as slowly as possible."

"As slowly as possible?"

"I'm not going to get bail, am I?"

"Not on these charges. Not when you're not a member of the community."

"I assume I'll be housed here in the jail until trial?"

"Yes."

He nodded. "So how slowly can you go?"

"If I drag my feet, you won't be arraigned until the day after tomorrow."

"Perfect. That's a great start. Please keep my wife informed."

· · ·

BETTY RICARDO PUT on her sunglasses as she walked out of the front doors of the county jail and down the sidewalk into the parking lot. When she got to her car, she set her briefcase on the hood and called Jodi Sutton.

"Hello?"

"Ms. Sutton?"

"Yes."

"This is Betty Ricardo. Your husband asked me to give you a message."

"He wants his court case stalled?"

"Yes. How did you know?"

"I know my husband. When's the arraignment?"

"Day after tomorrow."

"Thanks for calling."


JODI ENDED the phone call and looked out the front window of the little house they'd rented on Fish Creek Road, just west of town. Soybean field across the street. Corn behind them. Their nearest neighbor was two blocks away. The only time she'd seen another person here was when a school bus drove by, and it hadn't stopped on this section of road. She sat down on the sofa, opened an encrypted cloud account on her smartphone, and found Billy's phone number. Billy was their information and arms broker. A 10 percent guy, their go-to source for weapons, information, and job opportunities. She input his number. He answered on the first ring.

"Missus."

"Hey, Billy. I'm in a jam. I need a local connection in Putney, Ohio, to set me up inside the county jail and put me in touch with possible players."

"Okay. Might be a few hours. I'll call you back."

"Thanks."

She ended the call and called Chrissie. "Hey."

"Hey."

"What's your situation?"

"Just like you said, Terry called me up, crowing about catching the blackmailer. Told me we couldn't see each other anymore. At least not until after the election."

"Randy's in jail."

"I heard that. What are you going to do?"

"Not sure yet. Where do we stand?"

"You promised me thirty thousand dollars, but that money's gone. I'm in the clear, and I'm going to stay that way. No hard feelings. Good luck."

"Same to you." Jodi ended the call. That was a peculiar conversation. She'd never known anyone who missed a payday not to be mad about it. Even if they'd managed to escape undetected. Of course, Chrissie was an amateur. But maybe she was so calm because she already knew she wasn't going to get any money. Maybe she'd made a deal with Brighton behind their backs. And if that was the case, and she'd double-crossed them, then all bets were off. They'd post the video and screw her and Brighton at the same time. But even if Chrissie hadn't double-crossed them, Randy was in jail facing prison time, and as soon as she broke him out, they were going to make sure that Brighton lost his election.

CHRISSIE GOT up from her desk in the corner of her bedroom and put her phone in her back pocket. What a mess. At least she'd managed to stay in everyone's good graces. She hadn't gotten the $30,000, but she hadn't been arrested, Terry and Smith weren't after her, and she was pretty sure that Jodi believed her. Now all she had to do was keep her head down while Terry took his victory lap, and the FBI moved on to a new case. It was a shame about Randy, but he knew the risks. It wasn't her fault their plan failed. She got up and walked through to the kitchen to look in the refrigerator. What should she have for dinner?

She pulled out a bag of lettuce, a container of cherry tomatoes, a jar of olives, a block of cheddar cheese, and a container of deli chicken, putting them on the counter one at a time. Then she got out a dinner plate and started making a salad.

Her phone rang. She looked at the screen. Her mom. How was she doing?

"Hey, Mom."

"Hey, darling." Her mom spoke with an Eastern European accent. "How was your day?"

"Just another school day."

"Doing anything tonight?"

"Studying. How are things with you?"

"Fine. Everything's fine. We had turkey and mashed potatoes for dinner."

"I'm having a salad."

"Better for you. Listen, the reason I called is I wanted to get a sense of what's happening over the holidays."

"For Thanksgiving, there's no classes all week, so I'm going to come visit you. I'll stay at Becky's, because she'll be home, too."

"That sounds wonderful."

"Maybe Becky and I could cook, and I'd bring you to Becky's. Small group. Her parents, her brother, maybe one other friend. But we'll have to see. I haven't talked to Becky yet."

"Okay."

"And Christmas is still a little far away to plan, I think. I might have to stay here and work part of the time between semesters."

"But you'll come home at some point?"

"I hope so." Chrissie put the phone on speaker so that she could tear some lettuce onto her plate. "You sound good, Mom."

"I feel good."

"I'm glad," Chrissie said.

"Are you taking care of yourself? Getting enough sleep?"

"I'm fine, Mom, really."

"But there's no boyfriend."

"I don't have time."

"I was reading a magazine article that said when a person doesn't have a partner, things are not fine."

"They are for me."

"Which means butt out."

"Love you, Mom."

"Love you." Her mom ended the call.

Chrissie continued making her salad. On the phone, just now, her mom had been completely coherent. It was hard to believe that six months ago, when Chrissie had come home for spring break, she'd found packages stacked up by the door in the living room, rotting vegetables in the refrigerator, the sink full of dishes, and her mom yelling at the washing machine because she couldn't figure out how to turn it on. She'd managed to get her a doctor's appointment that week. It had taken until August to find a care facility to take her, and it took all her savings and the cash from the sale of her house to make the initial payment.

She put the salad items back in the refrigerator. The doctors said the dementia was progressive and would only get worse, but it was amazing how much difference a stable environment made.

# 4

_____

Randy sat on his cot in the two-man holding cell. The other occupant, a fat guy wearing a stained suit and the fearful expression of someone who had watched too many cop movies, was pacing from the back wall to the door like a bored panther at the zoo.

"How long have you been here?" Randy asked.

The man stopped walking. "Since last night."

"Have you been arraigned?"

"Yeah. I'm waiting for my lawyer to finish the paperwork to get me out of here. What about you?"

"No such luck for me."

"Really? What are you charged with?"

"Specifically? I think they're still making it up."

"What do they say you did?"

"They say I tried to blackmail the county prosecuting attorney, but it's complete bullshit."

"Whatever you say."

"What are you charged with?"

The man sat down on his cot. "Drunk driving. But you know how it is, I've got a clean record. My lawyer specializes in this sort of thing.

I'll end up on probation."

"Lucky you."

Randy lay down on his cot with his hands behind his head. He needed to relax, enjoy the quiet. This was as good as his life was going to be for a while. Once he was put into the general population, he'd have to be on his guard twenty-four seven, until he made a few friends and Jodi had a chance to find someone with connections inside the jail who could offer him protection.

MEANWHILE, Brighton and Smith stood between their vehicles in the parking lot of Memorial Park. Five people, three women and two men, were setting up a child's birthday party at a nearby shelter.

"Sutton's lawyer is stalling," Brighton said. "She's postponed the arraignment until the day after tomorrow."

"How's that a problem?" Smith replied. "Sutton's in jail. Maybe we just need to be patient."

"If she stalls every step of the way, the case will drag on into the new year. The longer it's open, the riskier it is for me. Someone might find out about Chrissie. We need him convicted as soon as possible."

"What do you have in mind?"

"What about his wife?" Brighton asked. "Can't we use her to pressure him?"

"With what? There's no proof she was involved. And she's gone into hiding."

"Which means she's guilty."

"We know she's guilty," Smith replied. "We just can't prove it without Chrissie's testimony."

"There's got to be some way to make him stop stalling."

"What if we start a rumor that he still has the blackmail money?"

"But he doesn't."

"Doesn't matter," Smith said. "He hid the money. We're claiming we got it back to save face and discourage other blackmailers."

"How will that help us?"

"If other inmates think he has the money, they're going to start pressuring him for a taste."

"Okay, I get it," Brighton said. "The convicts on the inside will go after him, and the criminals on the outside will go after his wife. And that will make him want to go to trial as quickly as possible."

"I hope so."

"How are you going to do this?"

"I'll talk to a friend at the sheriff's department. It'll take a few days, but word will start to trickle out."

"Keep me in the loop."

"You bet."

JODI WAS in a Koger grocery store, stocking up on toilet paper and canned goods, when her phone rang. It was Billy.

"I found your guy. Not much happening in Putney, Ohio, but the county is making bank off housing prisoners at their new, state-of-the-art county jail. Which means that getting contraband inside is a growth industry."

"So who is my guy?"

"Gerald Pappas. They call him Little Pap. His crew deals drugs into the jail."

"Can I trust him?"

"He's got a reputation for being a back-stabbing asshole, but he'll help you if your money's good."

"This is the best you could find?"

"There's another crew in town, but they're even worse."

"Okay. Where do I find him?"

"He works out of a bar that's outside the city limits. Appears to be a roadhouse sort of place. I've vouched for you via a friend, so Pappas ought to be approachable. I'll send an encrypted email of all the information I have."

"Thanks, Billy."

"Watch your back."

Two hours later, Jodi got out of her Cadillac Escalade in the gravel parking lot of a roadside bar called The Three Little Pigs. She was wearing a little black dress and carrying a small purse that contained a snub-nose revolver. A vintage neon sign featuring three cartoon pigs wearing chef hats lit up the front of the building. Inside, a long bar ran down the left side of the room, booths ran down the right side, and square tables sat in the space in between. Groups of men sat in the booths and at three of the tables. The only woman in the place was the bartender, a fiftyish brunette wearing a tight sweater.

Jodi crossed to the bar and sat on a stool. The bartender walked down to her.

"What'll you have?"

"Is Little Pap here?"

The bartender studied her face. "I haven't seen you before."

"That's because I'm not on the menu. I've got some business to discuss."

"We'll see. Through the door at the end of the bar."

Jodi pushed through a swinging door into a storeroom where two middle-age men and a topless blonde about half their age were sitting side-by-side on a sofa, playing a multi-person shooter game on a big screen TV. Cases of beer were stacked against one wall and an old desk with a landline phone on it sat in the back corner. The man to the right of the woman had a shaved head and a tightly trimmed salt-and-pepper beard. The man to the left was so fat his sweatshirt didn't cover his belly. They all stared at Jodi.

"Little Pap?"

The man on the right nodded.

"I'm Jodi Sutton. I was told you'd be expecting me."

Little Pap set down his game controller. "Jerry Jeff, you and Gwen get on out of here."

The woman pulled a white tank top over her head, and she and the fat man went out into the bar.

"Sorry to interrupt your game," Jodi said.

"No matter. What can I do for you?"

"I understand you're in charge of the jail."

He smiled. "Before we talk about my business, you're going to prove you're not wearing a wire."

"A guy you trust told you who I am."

"That's great for him. I have to know for myself. Take off the dress or leave."

She unzipped her little dress and stepped out if it. She stood in her black bra and panties with her arms down at her sides, her purse in her left hand. He made a twirling motion with his index finger. She turned in a circle.

"Thanks for humoring me."

"So we're done?"

"Yes."

She put her dress back on.

"Have a seat." He pointed at the end of the sofa.

She sat with her purse in her lap.

"What do you need?"

"You control the jail?"

"Yep."

"I want to arrange protection for my husband."

"Where is he now?"

"He's in a holding cell. He'll be arraigned the day after tomorrow."

"And he won't make bail?"

"No."

"When he moves into the general population, my guys will get in touch with him. In the yard and day room he'll sit with them."

"What'll that cost?"

"That depends."

"On what?"

"On your good will."

She batted her eyes. "What have you got in mind?"

He chuckled. "I don't want to fuck you, sweetheart. From the look of you, you know how to wrap a man around your finger. I don't want you trying to get inside my head. I want your cooperation. Favors for favors. Understand?"

She nodded.

"I need to know you understand. I don't want you baulking when I need you."

"So what do you want?"

"You're going to fuck Gwen while I watch. Then I'll know I can trust your word."

"The girl in the tank top?"

"Uh-huh."

"That's what she likes?"

"That's what I like, and she belongs to me."

"What if I say no?"

"Don't let the door hit you in the ass on your way out."

"I can't do something else?"

He shook his head. "You decide what help you need, and I provide it. I decide what you do in return, and you do it. Favor for favor."

She thought for a moment. Favor for favor. What did she want them to believe about her? She needed to convince them she was pliable, vulnerable, weak. Then she'd be able to start manipulating them. "Okay. You want to do this now or later?"

"Now."

"And my husband is taken care of?"

"I guarantee his safety, and around here my word is gold."

"We doing it in this room?"

"Naw, I've got a party room in the back." He gestured to a door on the far side of the storeroom.

"Then let's get it over with."

He led her into the back room. A king-size bed covered in a black sheet stood in the middle of the room. An old sofa and an armchair sat against the left wall. A sink in a Formica topped cabinet was situated against the righthand wall, with liquor bottles and glasses of various sizes clustered around it.

"You want a drink first?"

Jodi smiled. "I'm good." She took a deep breath and fell into that space where nothing mattered except achieving her goal.

Little Pap took a flip phone out of his shirt pocket. "Gwen, come on back."

After Gwen closed the door behind her, she grinned at Jodi, pulled her tank top off over her head, and tossed it onto the sofa—all without breaking stride—and then took Jodi in her arms and kissed her hard. Jodi spun her around on her heels, pushed her down on the bed, and climbed on top of her.

Little Pap sat down in an armchair to watch.

After they were finished and still lying naked side-by-side, Little Pap stood up from his chair and walked around the bed, studying them.

"I'm impressed," he said to Jodi. "I almost believed you were enjoying yourself."

"And my husband?"

"I'm a man of my word."

He walked over to the sink cabinet and took a cell phone out of the top drawer. "When you get a call, you answer it." He tossed the cell phone onto the bed beside her. "I've got business to attend to. You can take your time getting yourself together."

Little Pap left the room. Gwen rolled up on her side and put her hand on Jodi's belly. "You were enjoying yourself. You can't fool me."

"Didn't try to. Nothing wrong with mixing some pleasure with the business." She slid her arm under Gwen so that Gwen's head rested on her shoulder.

Gwen smiled. "Aw, we going to cuddle now? I'm not that easy to play."

"Smarter than you look?"

"Smart enough to give you some advice."

"Which is?"

"Pap will keep his word—until he doesn't."

"I expected as much."

"Then you won't be disappointed."

Jodi sat up. So Gwen was going to try to play her. Offering the obvious tidbit. If that was her opening gambit, she didn't stand a chance. But maybe that was the way in. Letting her think her ploy was working until it was time to turn her.

Jodi matter-of-factly put on her underwear while Gwen watched her from the bed. Then she stepped into her dress, smoothed it down, and picked up the cell phone. "See you around."

"What? No goodbye kiss?"

Jodi smiled. Gwen certainly had a lot of attitude. Was there some way to use that? Jodi went back through the storeroom to the front room. The bartender was drying glasses and putting them on the shelf under the counter. Little Pap was sitting at a table in the back, talking with Jerry Jeff. Jodi nodded toward him. He gave a little wave. She pushed through the front door and out into the parking lot. Favor for favor. Now she was going to find out how much new trouble she'd gotten herself into.

AFTER JODI LEFT, Gwen got dressed, went out into the bar, and sat down with Little Pap and Jerry Jeff.

"You did good," Little Pap said to her. "Got her thinking you're just eye candy."

"Thanks, Pap."

"Now you need to win her trust."

"Already working on it. What's the action?"

"The guy who vouched for them claims they're serious grifters. News report says he got busted on a blackmail. Did they keep any money? Did they keep any blackmail materials?"

"That's what you want to know?"

"That's what I want to know. You're on the woman. Jerry Jeff?"

"Yeah, boss."

"You work our contacts with the sheriff's department. If there's any money to be made here, we're going to make it."

"Why not just tax them for your help?" he asked.

"Because I want all of their money," Little Pap said.

"What if they don't like it?"

"We can dump her in the compost pit out on the farm, and he can get shanked in the jail."

· · ·

THE NEXT EVENING, Chrissie was in her bedroom getting dressed for an escort job. This was a weekly regular, an elderly man who took her to dinner at a white tablecloth restaurant, chatted about his day, and then took her back to his apartment where they lay together fully dressed on the bedspread of his bed and held hands while watching a Lawrence Welk Show rerun he'd recorded from public television. She'd showered, put on a cocktail dress, and was putting on her dinner date makeup when her escort phone rang.

"Chrissie?" Ms. Gleason asked.

"Yes."

"Mr. Brighton says that you're carrying some baggage."

"That's all settled."

"Is it? Then why is the FBI still watching you?"

"That's Brighton's fault."

"We know that, but until the FBI is finished with you, we can't use you."

"What about tonight?"

"No, I'm sorry. You get back in touch when the business with Mr. Brighton is finished."

"That could be months."

"Sorry, but we can't risk the exposure."

"But Mr. Sandlin is expecting me."

"No, he's not. I've sent someone else." Ms. Gleason ended the call.

Chrissie set her phone down and looked at herself in the mirror. What now? What could she do now? The bill from the care center came due at the end of every month. Nothing paid like escort work. She opened a package of makeup removal cloths and started wiping her face. Her savings would probably carry her through the rest of the semester. Then what? Terry and Smith were going to be watching her until Randy's trial was over and he was safely in prison. How long was that going to take?

She tossed the dirty makeup removal cloth into the trash and took out another one. Maybe she could find a waitressing job to tide her over. She wouldn't break even, but at least she wouldn't fall so far behind. Maybe they were hiring where her housemate Melanie worked. Goddamn Terry. Why was he pressuring Ms. Gleason? Why did he have to be such a bastard?

Two days later, at 9:30 a.m., Randy sat with Betty Ricardo at the defense table in courtroom three in the county courthouse. Tyler Motts, a Black man wearing a tailored suit, the assistant prosecutor assigned to the case, sat at the prosecutor's table, and Terry Brighton sat behind him, along with FBI agent Joe Smith.

The bailiff brought the room to order, and the judge, a middle-age woman with white hair, entered. Everyone sat, and the bailiff announced the case.

"This is the preliminary hearing," the judge said. She looked at Randy and Betty Ricardo. "How does the defendant plead?"

They stood up. Ricardo glanced at Randy. "Not guilty," he said.

The judge glanced at the court reporter. "Let the record show that the defendant entered a plea of not guilty. Now to the subject of bail."

Motts stood up. "Your honor, the defendant committed a serious crime and is a flight risk. It's the state's position that bail should be denied."

"Ms. Ricardo?"

"Your honor, my client is innocent of these charges and looks forward to his day in court. He should be granted bail or at least placed under house arrest pending trial."

Motts continued. "Your honor, we're not even really sure of the defendant's name. He does not appear to have any history at all, which makes it likely he will try to run if he gets the chance."

"Not using technology is not a crime," Ricardo replied.

The judge banged her gavel. "I've heard enough. The defendant will be held pending trial."

A sheriff's deputy took Randy back into custody. Motts stepped over to the defense table. "Ready to make a deal?"

Ricardo shook her head. "We're not making a deal. We're going to trial."

"You may want to talk with your client. Right now, before we've invested any time, no one got hurt and no gun was involved. We can offer three years—two and a half with good behavior. We go to trial, we win. That's ten years."

"My client is confident he'll be declared not guilty."

"Have it your way."

AFTER THE HEARING, Brighton and Smith stood together in the parking lot of the county courthouse in downtown Putney. Dark clouds were blowing in. People getting out of their cars were carrying raincoats for the showers forecast for after lunch. Brighton shoved his hands in his pockets. "Did you get the rumor out that Sutton still had the blackmail money?"

"Yes."

"Then it's not working. Sutton's still dragging out the process. Saying he wants to go to trial. That doesn't make sense."

"Give it some time."

"We need another tack, just in case the rumor doesn't work."

"What have you got in mind?"

"Is there any way to entangle his wife?"

"The only way to her is through Chrissie, remember? You didn't want to risk that."

"Not on the blackmail, but what if Chrissie found out something else we can use against her? She must be doing something illegal."

"How much pressure can I put on Chrissie?"

Brighton looked off across the street. Two lawyers were coming out of the Blue Bell diner. "Whatever it takes to get her involved with Mrs. Sutton."

BACK AT THE COUNTY JAIL, Randy was issued an orange jumpsuit and gym shoes and transferred from the holding cell into the general population, where he was placed in a cell with another prisoner. During the day, the cell doors were open. The prisoners were assigned to work teams, working in the kitchen or doing janitorial work. People who were not working sat in groups in the day room.

The cell contained two cots with a steel combination toilet and sink in between. The other prisoner in his cell was an older Black man with close-cropped white hair who limped when he walked. "I'm Carl," he said.

"I'm Randy."

"In this cell I'll back you, and I expect you to back me. But out there, I back my crew. You know how it is. Every color sticks together."

Randy nodded his head. "Fair enough. How long are you here for?"

"I'm overflow from the minimum-security prison. I've got six more years. I'll do it here or somewhere. What's your story?"

"Awaiting trial."

"Good luck with that." Carl lay down on his bunk and started reading a paperback western.

Randy went down the hall to the day room. A group of white prisoners sat in one corner, a group of Blacks in another, and a group of Latinos occupied some tables in the center. Randy hesitated for a moment, not quite sure if he should play independent or go over to the white group, when a muscled-up Black man with his sleeves of his jumpsuit rolled up on his biceps approached him.

"You Sutton?"

"Yeah. Randy Sutton."

"I'm Jamal. Your wife sends her regards. You sit with us."

THAT EVENING, Little Pap, Jerry Jeff, and Gwen were sitting at a table in the back corner of The Three Little Pigs. Business was slow. Only four other tables were occupied, and two men sat at the bar.

"So what have you found out?" Little Pap asked Jerry Jeff.

"Our guy at the sheriff's department says there's a rumor that the official report is bullshit, that Sutton managed to hide the ransom before he got caught."

"How much are we talking about?"

"One hundred thousand."

"That's real money." Little Pap looked from Jerry Jeff to Gwen. "If they had it, where would they hide it?"

"Can't put it in a bank," Jerry Jeff said. "And they don't know anyone around here. Maybe she's got it stashed at her house."

Little Pap turned to Gwen. "Have a look."

"I don't know where she's staying," Gwen replied.

"Can't we find out from the burner?"

Jerry Jeff shook his head. "She's got the GPS turned off."

"I could follow her," Gwen said.

Little Pap rubbed his chin. "We need to get her to trust us. Let's involve her in a job. Maybe that will cause her to feel like a part of our crew."

"What have you got in mind?" Gwen asked.

"We've been waiting for an opportunity to rob Osborne where we'd have some deniability. Tomorrow, we've got some business to discuss, so he'll be here for happy hour. You take Jodi with you and rob his place."

"Take her on a robbery? I don't know, Pap. That's a pretty big step."

"Supposedly she knows how to pick locks and work alarms. If she's all she's supposed to be, she'll be a lot of help. And if she's got no skills, well, chances are that the blackmail money shouldn't be so hard to find."


THE NEXT DAY, Randy and Jodi sat at a table in the far corner of the visitors' room at the county jail. There were three women, two with babies, sitting with other inmates, all spaced out in the room.

"I'm glad to see you," Randy said.

"Me, too. Your guys find you?"

"Yeah. It's the Black crew."

"That's surprising. The boss on the outside is cracker white."

"Doesn't matter one way or the other. You were moving faster than I expected."

"Thanks. Billy led me straight."

"What's it costing us?"

"Thus far? The boss is a perv. I had to take off my dress so he could 'check for a wire' and I had to have sex with his girlfriend while he watched, 'so he'd know he could trust me,' but he's saying favor for favor."

"Favor for favor. I don't like that. We're trying to stay out of trouble, not get in more. Anything else I should know?"

"Chrissie got away clean. Brighton didn't suspect a thing."

"That's hard to believe."

"I know. She didn't make any money, and she didn't seem surprised or angry. Makes me think that Brighton got to her somehow."

"Maybe he did. We can figure it out later." Randy tapped his fingers on the table. "That FBI agent and Brighton were at my hearing."

"Think he's Brighton's man?"

"It's the way my luck's been running."

"We'll just have to make do."

"Now that we've got Ricardo dragging out the pretrial, what's your next step?"

"The best time to break you out is while you're being transported to the courthouse in town."

"I agree."

"So I'm going to put together a plan to make that happen. I'm going to work fast, but it might take a month."

"Be careful. We've got a lot of balls in the air. Brighton, his pet FBI agent, Little Pap—any of them could upend our plans."

"Don't worry about it. I know what's at stake."

Randy glanced at the corrections officer standing by the door. "Highway ambush of a prisoner transportation van. That'll be tricky. There's not that much open country before you get into town, and once you're in town there's the usual cameras and people."

"Baby, I've got this. You just do what you've got to do to keep it together in here." She patted his hand. "See you in a week."


MEANWHILE, Chrissie shouldered her gym bag before she pushed through the glass door of the recreation center on campus and started down the sidewalk toward her house. Her phone vibrated in her pocket. She glanced at the screen. Overdraft alert. Shit. She still had money in her savings account, but she needed to move enough to her checking account to cover her bills if she wanted to avoid the overdraft fees.

No money coming in. She'd applied to some waitress jobs, but she hadn't heard back from any of them. None of her friends knew of any openings where they worked. And even if she could get a job, the hours were long, and the pay would be less than half of what she could make with just a few hours of escorting. She was using up her savings a lot faster than she thought she would. Maybe she needed to take out another student loan. God, it was depressing.

As she started down the hill to her house, she saw a black Ford Explorer parked on the street in front. Agent Smith. What could he want? He'd already ruined her life. Maybe she could just ignore him. She pretended the SUV wasn't there, but the passenger side window slid down and she heard Smith's voice calling to her.

"Ms. Makarova, I need a word."

She sighed.

"Get in."

She got in the passenger's side. "What's this about? I've done exactly what you told me. I'm not escorting. I've kept my mouth shut."

"Have you been in contact with Jodi Sutton?"

She shook her head. "She called me once. I told her Terry didn't suspect a thing and that I was out."

"I want you to tell her that you need back in."

"Why would I do that?"

"Because we want to know what she's up to."

"You need to find someone else."

"I don't have to find someone else. I've got you."

"What's in it for me?"

"Besides not being arrested for prostitution?"

"Please. That threat is all used up. You can't arrest me without ruining Terry's reputation. When word gets out about all the nasty stuff he likes, he'll be done."

"You find out anything of use to me, I'll pay you five hundred dollars."

"You'll pay me five hundred up front and another five hundred for any info."

"You're a piece of work." Smith reached into his pocket, took out a wad of cash, and peeled off five one-hundred-dollar bills. "This little job is a priority. I expect to hear from you in the next couple of days."

"I'm on the clock."

Chrissie got out of the SUV and walked up the steps to her front door. She grinned. Maybe this money would last until she could go back to escorting, especially if she got the extra $500. One thousand dollars would cover a whole month's bills. She glanced back at Smith's SUV before she opened her door. How would she get in touch with Jodi? Did she still have a phone number that worked? And what would she say that would convince her to tell her about whatever she was doing? She unlocked her door. She'd think of something. How about the truth? She was broke and needed money. She'd held up her end on the blackmail. If Randy and Jodi hadn't compromised the job by been photographed by Agent Smith, they would have gotten away with it. Jodi ought to trust her. Another $500. It couldn't be that hard.

# 5

Later that afternoon, Jodi got a text from Gwen on the burner phone.

*Meet me in the Kroger parking lot. Southwest corner.*

The Kroger grocery store parking lot was half-empty, the cars all parked near the entrance. Jodi spotted a Dodge Ram truck parked in the southwest corner. The surveillance camera mounted on the nearest light pole appeared to be broken. Jodi parked next to the Ram. Gwen lowered the window. "Get in."

Jodi got in the passenger's side of the truck. "What's up?"

"Little Pap has a job for us. Do you know how to pick locks?"

"Sure."

"Crack safes?"

"That's my husband's game. I can open a cheap one if it uses a key."

"Bypass alarms?"

"That depends. Alarm systems can be tricky nowadays."

"Then I guess we're going to have to be quick."

"So what's the job?"

"A guy owes the boss some money—gambling debts. He claims

he can't pay. The boss is tired of waiting. So we're going to go to his house and take what he owes."

"Why doesn't Little Pap just put a leg breaker on him?"

Gwen shrugged. "Little Pap does what he does. He says break into a house and steal what's owed, that's what we do."

"When are we doing this?"

"Now. While the guy's at The Three Little Pigs for happy hour."

"Have you got the tools?"

"Everything is in the bookbag in the floorboard."

Jodi looked in the bag. Throwaway gloves, lockpicks, black spray paint.

"You satisfied?"

She nodded.

"Put your seatbelt on."

Gwen drove out to a high-end subdivision on the north side of town. Two-story, three-car-garage brick houses with well-cared-for lawns lined the winding streets. There were no cars in the driveways, no children playing in the yards, no one walking on the sidewalks.

"Where is everyone?" Jodi asked.

"Parents are at work. Kids are in programs. That's why this is such a good time to come out here." Gwen gestured toward a tan brick house with yew bushes on either side of the front steps. "Here we are."

Gwen turned in the driveway and parked in front of the garage closest to the sidewalk. "You ready?"

Jodi nodded. She picked up the bookbag, took out the black spray paint, and slung the bag over her shoulder. She kept the spray paint down at her side as they walked up to the front door. As she came up off the top step, she covered her face with her free hand and spray-painted the front door camera. Then she dropped the paint can into the bookbag, took out the lockpicks, and picked the front door dead-bolt. Gwen pushed past her into the entryway. To the left was a dining room with a tall china cabinet and a long mahogany table; to the right was a living room with a sectional sofa and two matching chairs positioned around a glass-topped coffee table. In front of them, a wide staircase led up to the second floor. Jodi looked at the alarm pad on the wall by the door. It wasn't armed.

Gwen gestured toward the stairs. "Safe's up there."

They moved silently up the carpeted stairway and down the central hall. There were three doors on each side, all closed. Gwen opened the third door on the right side. It was a home office. Computer table, desktop computer, and an office chair were centered on the windows. To the left was a set of bi-fold closet doors. To the right were two easy chairs separated by a side table.

Gwen opened the closet doors. A file cabinet and shelves stacked with office supplies took up most of the space, but a two-foot by two-foot safe—a fireproof box, really—sat on the floor to the left. She turned to Jodi. "You're on."

Jodi squatted down in front of the safe. "Give me a minute." She inserted the lockpicks and scrubbed the tumblers. The bolt slid back. She opened the door.

Gwen put her hand on Jodi's shoulder. "Out of the way."

Jodi stood back while Gwen loaded the boxes from the safe into the bookbag. What was really going on here? This wasn't a debt collection.

"Hey!"

Jodi swiveled to the door. A big-bellied man wearing boxer shorts and holding a revolver stepped into the room. She sprang on him, grabbing for the gun as they fell back into the hall. The gun fired once, twice, three times as Jodi powered the man into the wall, pumping her legs into the floor, keeping him off balance. Both her hands gripped the man's gun hand, keeping it pointed up, while he punched wildly at her face. After he smacked into the wall, she head-butted him. His gun hand fell open as he slid toward the floor, and she snatched up the revolver.

"Fuck me," she said. She held the gun on the man and tried to catch her breath. "Don't move, asshole."

The man shook his head and then glared up at her from the floor. She glanced back at Gwen.

"He wasn't supposed to be here," she said.

"But he is."

"You two are dead," the man said. "You know that, don't you? You and everyone you love. Your only chance is to leave my stuff and get out of here, now."

"Watch him," Gwen said. She took her phone from her back pocket and stepped out of listening range.

The man continued. "I don't know you. I bet you're not from around here, but you look like you've got good sense. You don't want to get in the middle of this bullshit. Set the gun down and walk away. I don't ever see you again, you've got a pass."

Jodi studied the man. The place where he'd hit her over her left eye pounded like it was swelling. She felt like she'd been in a car wreck without a seatbelt. Fat guy, easy living, prison tattoos. Not afraid. This guy was a gangster or was protected by a gangster. His house was easy to rob because no one would be stupid enough to try.

Gwen came back down the hall, putting her phone into her back pocket. "We're getting out of here." She tossed the bookbag onto the floor. "Give me the gun."

Jodi handed her the revolver. She shot the fat guy twice in the chest and once in the head, wiped the gun on her shirt, and set it on the floor as she picked up the bookbag. "We need to hurry."

"Are you crazy? Why did you do that?"

"Because he'd seen us. It didn't matter what he said now, he was going to kill us first chance he got."

Jodi followed her out of the house and into the truck. Gwen backed out into the street and started away.

"So this was all bullshit from start to finish."

"He wasn't supposed to be there," Gwen replied.

"You sure about that?"

"We were just supposed to take his stash. Teach him a lesson is what Pap said."

"What do you think would have happened if I hadn't been lucky? If I hadn't caught him off guard and managed to get the gun?"

"Pap would have sorted things out."

"Pap would have lied and denied. We'd have been raped in every hole and beaten to death."

"That's not so."

"Grow up, little girl. You think your pussy is so special? He'd be holding tryouts for your job before they even found our bodies."

"Be quiet," she snapped. "We're not having this conversation."

Jodi shook her head. Gwen was either an idiot or one of the best con artists Jodi had ever seen, and she didn't believe that for a second. Go to a job not knowing what's what. Relying on Little Pap—who wasn't even there—to sort it out. She was lucky she wasn't already in a landfill.

Gwen stopped in the Kroger parking lot behind Jodi's car. "Here you are."

"Think about what I said. You need to take care of yourself."

"Get out of my truck."

Jodi got into her Escalade. Gwen was loyal, she'd give her that. What did Little Pap have on her? Little Pap didn't have the kind of charisma that inspired followers—not the kind who would die or go to jail for him. And Jodi knew Little Pap would sell her out in a minute. The dead man's crew would be out for blood. What has Billy said? That the other crew was even worse than Little Pap. At least she and Gwen hadn't been seen leaving the house, and they hadn't left any evidence behind.

She pulled out of her space and drove around the nearby neighborhood, making sure she wasn't being followed before she headed back to the safehouse. That robbery had been a clusterfuck. But maybe, just maybe, she could use it to start turning Gwen against Little Pap. One thing was for sure. She needed to spring Randy, and they needed to get out of this town before Little Pap got her into a mess she couldn't get out of.

GWEN PARKED her truck by the dumpster behind The Three Little Pigs and went in the back door to the storeroom. Little Pap was sitting behind his desk in the corner, and Jerry Jeff was sitting in a side chair, both drinking whiskey.

"There she is," Little Pap said. He poured her a whiskey and pushed it across the desk toward her. She set the bookbag down on the desk, but she didn't pick up the glass of whiskey or sit down in the other side chair. She just stood there with her arms crossed.

"I know you're pissed off," Little Pap continued. "But everything worked out in the end."

"You told me that Osborne wouldn't be there."

"That's what we thought. Isn't that right, Jerry?"

"That's right."

"Then why didn't you call me when he didn't show up here?" she asked.

Little Pap shrugged. "We didn't know where he was. We thought he was running late, that he'd turn up any minute. No one was as surprised as me when you called."

"Motherfucker." She picked up the glass of whiskey and drained it. Little Pap poured her another.

"Sit down," he said.

She sat down and reached for her fresh drink. "If it hadn't been for Jodi, I'd be dead now."

"No, she'd be dead. Our story would be that it was her play, that she led you astray, that you didn't realize what she was up to until Osborne walked into the room. You didn't know it was his house."

"You think they would have believed it?"

"Believe it or not, they'd have to accept it. Drink up, darling."

He opened the bookbag, took out one of the boxes, opened it, and took out a banded bundle of cash, which he tossed to Gwen. "There's your cut and something extra. You showed initiative. You turned mud into gold."

She thumbed through the money.

"So relax," he continued. "It's all good. No one's going to find out what happened."

"What about Jodi? She's pissed off at us now."

"Not much chance of winning her over in the short run. So find out where she lives, but don't let her spot you. If she's got the blackmail money, we're going to take it."

LATER THAT EVENING, Chrissie was sitting at her desk in her bedroom, reading a textbook on her laptop, but she couldn't focus. There was no putting off calling Jodi. She'd been paid. She needed to get it done. Chrissie looked in the received phone calls on her phone, found the last call from Jodi, set her phone to record the call, and tapped the number. It rang eight times but didn't switch to voicemail. Chrissie was about to end the call when she heard Jodi's voice.

"Hello?"

"Jodi, this is Chrissie."

"I'm surprised to hear from you."

"I'm surprised this number still works."

"Why are you calling?"

"I know how I left it, but I'd like to reconsider."

"Why?"

"I'm broke. I can't escort right now. Terry's seen to that."

"I'm sorry to hear that, but I don't know what it has to do with me."

"Have you got anything going on? Anything at all? Anything that you might need a partner or just a helper on? I'm really desperate."

"I don't have anything going right now, but if something comes up, I'll keep you in mind."

"Nothing?"

"I'm sorry." Jodi ended the call.

Well, Chrissie thought, she'd tried her best. She played back the recording. The conversation was all there. If Agent Smith questioned what she'd done, she'd be able to prove she'd done her best. And even if she wouldn't make another $500, maybe the recording would get him off her back.

.  .  .

JODI STOOD at her front window, looking out at the road, one hand holding an ice pack to her swollen eye, the other hand holding her phone. No one was parked within sight of the house. She actually did need some help—someone to help with surveillance on her plan to break Randy out of jail—but there was no way she was going to trust Chrissie, not when she wasn't sure if she ratted them out to Brighton on the blackmail. Besides, there was too much at stake to take a chance on anyone who wasn't a professional. Chrissie's skills were all in sex work. In any other game, she'd be even less reliable than Gwen, and that was saying something. No, the only person she could trust was Randy. And with him in jail, she was on her own.

THE NEXT DAY, Randy was lying on his cot after lunch when Jamal came into the cell.

"Knock, knock," he said.

Randy sat up. "What's up?"

"Where's Carl?"

"Don't know."

Jamal unzipped his jumpsuit and took a plastic bag out of the front of his underwear. "Need you to do a favor."

"No disrespect, but I don't want to get involved in your business."

"Me neither. I'd rather lay around and have people do for me, but that's not how it works. You need my protection. I need your help."

Randy took the bag. "What is it?"

"What do you think? Give it to the white boy with the swastika on his cheek."

"The guy with the shaved head?"

Jamal nodded. "He's usually hanging out with his guys right now, so wait a little bit. And don't give it to him in the day room. Too many cameras."

"So where then?"

"You figure it out."

Jamal drifted back down the hall.

Randy put the bag in his underwear. Drugs—he didn't care if

people took them, but bad things happened to people who used drugs, and he didn't want to be involved in any way. He walked down the hallway toward the day room. He'd expected that he'd have to help Little Pap with his contraband business, but he thought he'd get a little more time to settle in. And drugs were the worst thing to get caught with.

Up ahead, he saw Swastika Cheek in the hall, talking with two white guys with crewcuts and tattooed hands.

"Hey," he said.

The two guys turned toward him, blocking his path. "We got nothing for a race traitor," the closest one said.

"Go back to the monkeys," the other one added.

"I don't have any business with you two," Randy said. "I just need a word with your buddy."

Swastika Cheek pushed through the other guys. "You go on. I'll catch up."

The other guys ambled off. Swastika Cheek turned to Randy. "Only one reason you're looking for me."

Randy glanced down the hall to the surveillance camera mounted near the ceiling. It was pointed directly at Swastika Cheek's back. Randy unzipped his jumpsuit and took the plastic bag out of his underwear. Swastika Cheek palmed it.

"You the new distribution guy?"

"I guess that's me."

"When's the next drop?"

"That I don't know. I'll be in touch when I've got something."

"Stay out of the way if my guys get argumentative. People don't beef much in here 'cause the living is easy, but things can turn bad just like that." He snapped his fingers.

Randy went back to his cell. Carl was lying on his cot, reading a *Newsweek*. "They got you slinging drugs."

"Just doing what I've got to do."

"You'd be better off taking your lumps. People act tough in here, but nobody they let in here is tough."

"I'll keep that in mind."

"You do that."


AGENT SMITH'S Explorer was parked in front of Chrissie's house when she came home from class. She walked up the passenger's side and climbed in. "What's up?"

"Did you call Mrs. Sutton?"

"Yes."

"What did she say?"

She took out her phone. "I recorded it."

She played the conversation back.

"So she turned you down flat?"

"You heard the recording."

"You need to try again."

"Try again? She not going to change her mind."

"She's not her husband. You beg enough, she'll give in."

"I don't think she will."

"You're still going to try. Give her a few days, then try her again."

"It's a waste of time."

"So waste your time. You've been paid."

"Anything else?"

He shook his head.

Chrissie got out of the car. What a pain in the ass. At least he hadn't asked for his money back. Maybe he was right. Maybe Jodi would tell her something valuable. Maybe she'd be able to claim another $500. But there was no way she was going to get involved in any job Jodi was planning. That's how she ended up in this mess in the first place. That's where she drew the line. She was going to stay out of trouble and get paid. That was her plan.

# 6

---

Over the next few days, Jodi swapped out rental cars and drove out to the county jail at 7:00 a.m., where she parked on the shoulder of the road and used binoculars to watch for the sheriff's prisoner transportation van to arrive and load up prisoners going to the courthouse. Monday through Friday, the van always arrived at about 8:40 a.m., loaded some prisoners, and took exactly the same route into town to the courthouse.

There were two spots suitable for an ambush. One was where the county road ran through a grove of oak and hickory trees before a small bridge over a creek, and the other was just inside the city limits, at an abandoned gas station on the other side of a double set of railroad tracks. Either spot required two cars to box in the van, which meant two drivers and at least two other guys for the probable gunfight with the deputies in the van.

So four guys and two vehicles and the van might still outrun them. They'd only get one chance. After that the sheriff's department would be expecting trouble. Stealing two vehicles for the ambush would be easy, but getting four guys for a job where there was no money to be made? She had less than $17,000 left. That wasn't enough to pay four guys to get into a gunfight with the sheriffs and still have enough money to run on after they freed Randy.

She sat back on the sofa in the safehouse, her laptop on her thighs, going over the route from the jail to the courthouse, letting her mind float. How could she do this job by herself? Have to stop the van. Have to deal with the driver and the guard. What if she could get control of the van, make it go where she wanted it to go? Crash it into a tree. Drive it into a ditch. Get the element of surprise. The sheriff's prisoner transportation van was new, full of electronics—it was essentially a computer on wheels. Was there a way to gain control of it?

She called Billy. "Can you get me a computer tablet that can remotely control the computer of a Ford utility van so that I can override the driver and drive the van from a distance?

"Sorry. Cars can't be hacked like that anymore. That window closed after those White Hat hackers made videos overriding drivers and posted them on YouTube."

"You sure?"

"Only way to do it now is to physically install an override device on the car's computer, so that you're controlling the car with a remote, like it's a model car."

"Can you send me the tech to do that?"

"Anything else?"

"Two full sets of gear."

"Rifles, pistols, and Kevlar vests?"

"Yes. And a tranquilizer dart gun."

"Catch and release?"

"Something like that."

"It'll take three to four days."

"Thanks."

She ended the call. Now she had to find a way to install the override device on the sheriff's transport van. Where did the sheriff's department get its vehicles serviced? She did a Google search on her laptop.

The county had its own vehicle maintenance department, which maintained the county trucks and cars, as well as the sheriff's department vehicles. The next morning, at 7:30 a.m., she drove down to the maintenance facility, located across from the fenced-in motor pool where the county trucks and cars were parked, and watched the employees come in to work. Both the men and the women wore dark blue pants, light blue shirts, work boots, and ball caps or stocking caps.

At 8:00 a.m., a sheriff's department cruiser parked outside the facility, and two deputies got out. They strode into the motor pool parking lot and drove out in the prisoner transport van. She followed them out to the county jail, where they drove through the gate to the loading dock. She pulled over on the shoulder of the road and acted as if she was looking at a map on her phone. Thirty minutes later, the van drove around to the other side of the jail and loaded up four prisoners. She followed the van along the usual route to the county courthouse.

She went out to the maintenance facility three days in a row, driving different rental cars, wearing different wigs, and parking in different spots. Every day was the same. Two deputies got out of a cruiser. They left in the prisoner transportation van and drove out to the county jail. Some days they drove to the loading dock around the side of the building, and on others they drove straight to the prisoner loading door. But thus far, every day they picked up the van from the motor pool in the morning, which meant that maybe she could access the van in the motor pool parking lot during the night and install the car computer override device. If she could figure out how to do it. That would usually be Randy's job.

At lunchtime, back at the safe house, while Jodi was sitting at the kitchen table eating a tuna salad sandwich, her phone rang. It was Chrissie again. Jodi finished chewing and took a drink of water before she answered the phone. "I thought I made myself clear."

"Please, Jodi, I've got nowhere else to turn. I really, really, really need a job. If you don't need any help, do you know someone who does?"

"Chrissie, my priority right now is to stay out of trouble so that I can help Randy. I've got nothing going on, and I don't know anyone who is doing anything. Goodbye." She ended the call.

Chrissie was so contrite, so willing, so obviously wanting to lure her in. It seemed more and more likely that Chrissie was working for Brighton and the FBI guy. Not that it mattered. She already had to keep an eye out for them as well as Little Pap's people. They were much more likely to be able to disrupt the jail break. And that was something she couldn't allow. She drank her iced tea and took her glass and plate to the dishwasher.

The next morning, while waiting for the deputies to arrive, she saw a pickup truck park on the street on the left side of the maintenance facility. She took out her binoculars. Jerry Jeff sat behind the wheel. She scooted down in her seat. What was he up to?

He squeezed out of the truck. He was dressed like a vehicle maintenance worker, except he wore gym shoes instead of work boots. He had the strap to a duffel bag over one shoulder. Jodi reached across to the glove box to get her digital camera and snapped his picture. He went into the maintenance facility and came out in a few minutes with an unshaven Latino mechanic. As they crossed into the parking lot, Jodi took another photo.

Jodi got out of her car and walked up to the fence surrounding the parking lot, keeping an eye on Jerry Jeff and the mechanic. They stopped at the prisoner transportation van, but she couldn't see what they were doing. A few minutes later, they left the parking lot without the duffel, the Latino going back into the maintenance facility and Jerry Jeff getting back in his truck. When the deputies arrived, he waved at them and then drove off.

Jodi followed the transport van out to the county jail, where it pulled up to the loading dock. She sat on the side of the highway with her binoculars and watched as a corrections officer came out of the loading dock door and one of the deputies handed him the duffel bag. *So that's how contraband gets into the jail.* She drove back into town, changed out her rental car and her wig, and went back to the county vehicle maintenance facility. When the unshaven Latino left work at 3:30 p.m. in a Ford pickup truck, she was following him.

He pulled up the driveway of a white, one-story, one-car garage house on a street of similar houses and went inside. Jodi turned around at the end of the block and parked across the street where she had a good view of the front of the house. A few minutes later, a school bus stopped at the corner, put out its stop sign, and opened its door. Several grade-school age children got out, their coats open, school bags over their shoulders, and started down the sidewalk, jostling and shouting. Two boys went into the mechanic's house. Jodi took photos of the truck's license plate and the front of the house.

After she got home, she got on her computer and opened an illegal program that could trace the truck's license plate number and reveal the name of its owner. It was someone named Victor Lopez. She cross-checked the name against the county property records. The small, white, single-story house was his. He was helping to move contraband into the jail. He had two kids, probably a wife as well—a life definitely worth protecting. She smiled to herself. She wasn't going to have to risk being caught in the motor pool parking lot while she was fumbling to install the computer override. This family man was going to do it for her.

That evening she got a call from Billy. "I've got your gear for you. Go down to the rest stop south of town. Look for a silver Suburban driven by an Asian guy with a ponytail."

"Including the car computer override?"

"Everything."

"Thanks, Billy."

Jodi drove down to the rest stop. The semitruck side of the rest stop was packed with parked trucks, while the car side contained only three vehicles, a Camry and a Sentra parked in front of the doors to the visitors' center, and a silver Suburban parked at the far end of the lot. Jodi backed into a spot beside the Suburban. An Asian guy wearing a flannel shirt with the sleeves rolled up got out of the Suburban and came up to Jodi's window.

"Billy sends his regards. I've got your gear in the back."

Jodi popped the liftback and went around to the back of the Escalade. The Asian guy used his fob to open the liftback on the

Suburban. Three black duffel bags, two large and one small, sat in a row in the back. The guy moved them into the back of the Cadillac one at a time.

"Good luck," he said. He got back in the Suburban and drove away.

Jodi unzipped the duffels. The two large ones each contained an AR-15 rifle, a SIG Sauer pistol, a Kevlar vest, and several boxes of ammunition. The small one contained a six inch by six inch electronic device, a small tablet remote controller, and a dart pistol with a box of darts. Everything she needed. It was time to put her plan into play.

Gwen sat on the shoulder of the rest stop entrance ramp and watched the Suburban drive away. When Jodi pulled out of her parking space, Gwen turned on her headlights and started after her. She'd been lucky to spot her at a crossroads on the other side of Putney and follow her down here. Maybe tonight she'd find out where she lived. She drove by the visitors' center and followed Jodi down the exit ramp and onto the freeway, staying several cars back. The sun had already fallen behind the far hills and the sky was rapidly darkening, which would make it harder for Jodi to spot her.

She followed Jodi down the first exit ramp into Putney, taking the state highway around the perimeter of the university. So far, so good. The night was overcast, and the streetlights were far apart, but she let Jodi get seven or eight car lengths ahead just in case. They turned right onto Luthor Parkway, heading for the Putney State University football stadium. Then Jodi put on her turn signal, pulled into a McDonald's restaurant, and got in line at the drive-through.

Gwen drove by, turned around in a parking lot, drove back to the McDonald's, and pulled into a parking space where she could watch the end of the drive-through. A few minutes later, Jodi's Cadillac appeared and took a right back onto Luthor Parkway. Gwen followed. The traffic was getting busier. Gwen moved in closer. At the next intersection, Jodi shot through the traffic lights just as they changed to red.

Gwen was surrounded by traffic three cars back. When the traffic lights turned green, she sped up the parkway, passing cars on the left and right, looking for Jodi's Cadillac, but she was gone. Damn it. Had Jodi spotted her at the McDonald's, or was she already onto her when she pulled in there? Maybe she hadn't spotted her at all. Maybe she always pushed the traffic lights. One thing was for sure. She couldn't tail her by herself. She needed two cars.

Meanwhile, Smith and Brighton sat in a booth in the back of a Macy's Lounge, a small bar sandwiched between a jewelry store and a shoe store downtown. Three men sat at the bar watching a football game, and a couple sat in a table up by the front window. Smith and Brighton were both nursing tap beers.

"So you made Chrissie ask twice?" Brighton asked.

Smith nodded. "She made a recording the first time. Jodi Sutton turned her down flat. So I told her to try again. Same result."

"So she's not doing anything that we could use against her?"

"We don't know," Smith replied. "We just know she doesn't need help, or she doesn't trust Chrissie."

"Is there any other way we can find out what she's up to?"

"Not without involving a lot of manpower for surveillance. We'd have to be on her twenty-four seven until we knew what to look for."

"Damn it."

"I know. You're just going to have to wait it out. Maybe the black-mail money rumor will lead to something."

"I doubt it." Brighton glanced at his watch and stood up. "Well, it was worth a try. Thanks for your help."

"You bet."

Jodi drove around a neighborhood north of the university, making sure she'd lost whoever was following her, before she drove out to the industrial area west of town to Bob's Self Storage, six rows of white, concrete block storage garages with gravel alleys between them. She drove down the second gravel alley until she reached her storage garage. She unlocked the garage door and raised it. The space inside, the size of a one-car garage, was empty. She drove the Escalade inside, locked the garage door, walked out to street, and got into a rented Honda CR-V.

THE NEXT MORNING at the county jail, when Randy was on his way back to his cell after breakfast, Swastika Cheek's two buddies were waiting for him in the hall, their tattooed hands balled into fists.

"What's up?"

The nearest one punched him in the side of the head, knocking him back into the wall. The second one stepped up to him and grabbed him by the front of his orange jumpsuit.

"We hear you got money."

"I don't know what you're talking about."

"Wrong answer." He punched Randy in the stomach. Randy doubled over, clutching his belly.

"We hear you've got blackmail money. That the cops didn't get it. So you got taxes to pay."

"How am I going to do that?"

"You figure it out." He pushed Randy to the floor and kicked him. Then he tapped his buddy on the shoulder and they walked away.

Randy climbed up the wall to get to his feet and stumbled down the hall to his cell. Bastards. Why did they think he had money? It didn't make sense. He put his hand on the doorframe as he turned into his cell. Carl wasn't there. He lay down on his cot. But it didn't have to make sense. Not with those two. IQ of thirty on a warm day. He'd have to be more careful about wandering around in the halls by himself.

. . .

MEANWHILE, Jodi followed Lopez from his house to the county vehicle maintenance facility. At noon, he left work and drove to a Stop & Go convenience store and went inside. Jodi parked beside his truck and got out of the Honda CR-V with the small duffel over her shoulder. When he came out with a bottle of iced tea and a bag of snacks, she approached him.

"Victor Lopez?"

He looked her up and down.

"Let me show you some pictures." She reached into the duffel and handed him copies of the photos she'd taken the previous day.

He glanced through them. "These don't mean anything."

"They mean that you're helping Little Pap move contraband into the county jail. You, Jerry Jeff, and the two deputies who drive the van."

"Bullshit."

"Hey, I don't care if you're picking up a few extra dollars. Matter of fact, I'd like to pay you to do some work for me."

"Not interested."

"Be a shame for your boys to grow up without their dad. You're already in the game. At any time, you might get caught."

"You threatening me?"

"Not at all. Just telling you the truth. If the county sees these photos, they'll fire you just to be on the safe side."

He glanced around the parking lot. "How do I know you're not a cop?"

"If I was a cop, I wouldn't be by myself, and we'd be having this talk at the county jail."

"I could say yes, take your money, and do nothing."

"And I could burn your house down just for the pleasure of watching you run out into the dark."

He rubbed his chin. "You've got some big balls on you."

"Just trying to give you some money."

"Okay. What's the job?"

"I'll pay you three thousand dollars to install a bit of electronics onto the computer of the prisoner transportation van."

"What kind of electronics?"

"A computer override."

"You planning to control the van remotely?"

"Maybe."

"I'd have to dig into the console pretty far. Make it five thousand."

"How about four thousand?"

He shook his head. "Five thousand."

"Five thousand it is. How soon can you do it?"

"Can't just pull the van into the shop. I need a week at least to fit it into the schedule."

"Okay. A week." She handed him the duffel. "The computer override and its controller are in here."

He took out the electronic device and turned it over in his hand. "I need half the money up front."

"I'll give you two thousand right now."

"Okay."

She went to the passenger's side of the Honda, opened the door, and bent down over the passenger's seat to take $2,000 out of a manilla envelope and put it in a smaller envelope. Then she came back around the SUV to where Lopez was standing.

"I expect this job to be done right."

"It'll be done right."

She handed him the smaller envelope, and then took a business card with a phone number on it out of her pocket and handed it to him. "Call this number when the work is done."

## 7

Two days later, Jodi sat with Randy at a table in the back corner of the visitors' room at the county jail. She glanced nonchalantly at the other visitors and the corrections officer standing in the doorway before she spoke.

"How did you get that black eye?"

"White power guys think I have the blackmail money."

"Wonder who started that rumor?"

"Brighton? Agent Smith? Maybe no one. People in here got all day to let their imaginations run wild."

"I thought Little Pap's guys were supposed to protect you."

"Didn't want to get them involved. They've got me doing favors, and I don't want to owe any more than I have to."

"Well, you won't be here much longer."

"Really?"

"Yes." She explained her plan.

"So you'll have the computer override set in five more days?"

"I should."

"You certain the tech is going to work?"

"Yeah. As certain as you can be about these things."

"Okay. I'll get Ricardo to set up a hearing at the courthouse in nine or ten days."

"On what basis?"

"I'm going to change my plea."

"Then my plan better work."

"Either it works, or we need a new plan."

She nodded. "Okay. Expect the unexpected when I take over the driving."

"Anything else I need to know about?"

She told him about the fouled-up robbery.

"Little Pap really is a top caliber asshole," he said. "Has he asked you to do anything else?"

"Not yet."

"Stall him if you can."


Gwen turned at the crossroad and drove toward the visitors' parking at the county jail. She hoped she wasn't too late. She'd rushed to her Camry and sped across town from The Three Little Pigs after she'd gotten the phone call from the corrections officer at the visitors' sign-in. And there Jodi was, coming out of the front doors of the county jail and walking toward the visitors' parking. Gwen smiled to herself. Her luck was holding out. She pulled onto the shoulder of the road and waited as Jodi got into a Honda CR-V, pulled out of the jail parking lot, and headed toward town.

Gwen fell in behind her, staying well back on the county road. This was the only direct route into town, so there wasn't much risk of losing her. She picked up her smartphone and called Jerry Jeff. "We're coming into town on Pollock Road. She's driving a white Honda SUV."

She closed in as Jodi crossed the railroad tracks at the edge of town. Up ahead, Jerry Jeff was sitting in an old pickup truck in front of a boarded-up gas station. When Jodi drove by, he pulled out and started after her. Gwen took a right turn and then a left to follow on a parallel street.

Traffic picked up when Jodi turned onto King Boulevard. Jerry Jeff stayed three cars back. When Jodi pulled into a Kroger grocery store parking lot, Jerry Jeff continued to the next intersection and turned right into a Caffeination coffee shop, where he parked with a good view of the street.

Gwen pulled into the Koger and parked where she could watch the Honda. About thirty minutes later, Jodi came out of the store carrying two bags. Gwen followed her until she was three blocks past the Caffeination, where Gwen fell back and let Jerry Jeff take over.

At the next intersection, Jodi got into the left turn lane. A BMW pulled in behind her, and Jerry Jeff pulled in behind the BMW. The car in front of Jodi turned left and then the light turned red. At the first gap in the cross-traffic, Jodi shot through the red light. Jerry Jeff was trapped behind the BMW. The light changed. Jerry Jeff took the left turn and then the first right. He raced up a parallel street through a residential area. Gwen drove straight through the intersection, noted the Honda about a block ahead, and carefully closed the distance to three cars. Gwen called Jerry Jeff. "She must have made you. Stay on the side street."

Jodi continued until the houses thinned out west of town, where she pulled into the driveway of a little ranch house surrounded by farm fields. Gwen drove by without slowing down. She called Jerry Jeff. "Found her house. She's on Fish Creek Road past the first inter- section, but there's nowhere to sit where we can watch for her to leave. Get a new car and sit at the intersection. I'll be down the road on the other side. When she leaves, she'll have to go one way or the other."

Gwen pulled off the road at the gate to a farm field. How long was this going to take? She got out her phone to look at her Instagram. Thirty minutes later, Jerry Jeff called. "I'm in a red Mazda. The CR-V is still parked at the house and I'm back at the intersection."

Gwen looked at her email. She wished she had a cup of coffee. An hour later, a school bus drove by. At dusk, she got another call from Jerry Jeff. "She just drove past me."

"Follow her. Let me know when she heads back to her house."

Gwen drove down to the little house and parked in the gravel driveway. The outside lights over the front door were on. She walked up onto the stoop and knocked. No one answered. She knocked again. No barking, no footsteps. She tried the doorknob. It turned. The hair went up on the back of her neck. Was it a trap? She eased the door open an inch. What was she expecting? A boobytrap? That was crazy. She walked into the room and closed the door behind her. Had Jodi left the door open on purpose? No matter, she wasn't going to leave any indication that she'd been here. The living room contained a sofa, side chair, coffee table and TV. No cabinet or closet to hide $100,000.

She walked down the short hall to the bedroom, searched the dresser and the closet, checked the pockets of the hanging clothes, and felt under the mattress. No money. In the bathroom she looked in the medicine cabinet over the sink. In the eat-in kitchen, she looked through the cabinets, the refrigerator, even the stove. Nothing.

There was a hatch to the attic in the hall. She stood on a kitchen chair to reach the pull cord to the folding stairs. Then she climbed up and turned on the single light bulb. Rafters and blown-in insulation that hadn't been touched in years. She closed the hatch and put the kitchen chair back. There was no money hidden inside the house. She went outside and looked for a door to the crawl space under the house. It was at the back of the house next to the outside water spigot. She got down on her hands and knees, opened the door and peeked into the gloom. She couldn't see anything. She waved her hand inside, found the pull string for a light and turned it on. Some garden tools were piled within reach. Otherwise, it was cobwebs and dirt. She turned off the light and shut the door. Waste of time. She called Jerry Jeff. "Nothing here."

"You sure?"

"Absolutely."

"Pap isn't going to like it."

"I know. Meet me back at the Pigs."

. . .

JODI SAT at a table along the inside wall of Buddy's Chicken Shack. The restaurant was busy, which is why she chose it. Families with children took up most of the tables and the TVs mounted on the walls showed football games or a sports commentary show. She was eating a chicken sandwich with a spinach salad and drinking a tap beer. Little Pap's people ought to be finished searching her house by the time she got back. What were they looking for? Could they possibly be stupid enough to believe she'd leave anything valuable or important at the house? Had they heard the rumor about the blackmail money? Did they think she had it? She'd tipped Jerry Jeff that she'd known he was following her. Did Gwen believe she didn't know about her?

She finished her beer. She needed to find a new safehouse using a new ID, someplace no one would know about that she and Randy could run to after the jailbreak. Set it up and then stay away from it. Little Pap was a snake. He would double-cross them for sure if he thought there was anything to gain. She motioned to her server. "Check, please."

THE PARKING LOT at The Three Little Pigs was full when Gwen pulled into the lot, so she parked around the side of the building. Inside, Country Top 40 was blasting from the jukebox and the waitress was squeezing through the tables carrying a full tray of bottled beers and mixed drinks. Gwen spotted Little Pap at his table in the back. Jerry Jeff was already sitting with him. Gwen wove through the tables and sat with her back to the door.

Little Pap turned to her. "You didn't find anything?"

She shook her head. "Nothing. Just women's clothes and the stuff you find in a furnished rental."

"Maybe I should send someone else."

"There's nothing in the attic, nothing under the floor, nothing in any closet or cabinet, nothing in the pockets of any clothes. No money and no lockbox key."

Jerry Jeff cut in. "That doesn't mean there won't be something in there in a week."

"She's not going to leave anything there, I don't think."

"You think she's keeping it in her car?" Jerry Jeff asked.

"That would be crazy," Gwen replied.

"Well, she wasn't driving the Escalade."

Little Pap continued. "She didn't spot you?"

"Not me. Thought she'd ditched Jerry Jeff."

"We played it sweet, boss," Jerry Jeff added. "No way she spotted Gwen."

"Randy can't stay in that jail forever," Little Pap said. "No matter how slow his case is moving, he's going to go to trial in the next few months or so. After that, he'll be out on the street or in the state pen, and we'll have missed our chance."

"So what do you want to do?" Gwen asked.

"Jodi is a careful girl. If she's still spooked from that business with Osborne, she'll be on high alert. Maybe Jerry Jeff's right. Maybe the money will turn up later. Let's give her a little time to settle down, and then we'll have another look."


THE NEXT AFTERNOON, Jodi went into While You Wait Computer Repairs, located on a side street adjacent to the downtown shopping strip. Shelves of used computers, screens, and laptops ran along the left wall. Two straight-backed chairs and a coffee table loaded with computer magazines sat on the right side of the room. Jodi went back to the counter. A thirty-something man with a ring in one nostril and long hair combed down one side of his face looked up from a cell phone that lay open on the glass countertop.

"What can I do for you?"

"I'm looking for Tank."

"Speaking."

"Billy sent me."

Tank nodded. "What do you need?"

"Driver's license associated with an existing bank account and social security number."

"How many?"

"Just one."

"You know all that info is hot, right? It'll only be good until the account owner calls it in. So I make no guarantee about how long the ID will work."

"The driver's license hasn't been used yet, has it?"

"No."

"Then we're good."

"You want the physical driver's license as well?"

She nodded.

"I can make you a card. It probably won't fool the cops, but no one else will be able to tell the difference."

"You sure about that?"

"College town. I make a ton of them for underage drinkers."

"Good enough."

"You got a photo?"

"No."

"Come on into the back. I've got a camera set up with a driver's license background."


MEANWHILE, Smith stepped into Brighton's office at the county administrative building and closed the door behind him. "What's up?"

Brighton sat back in his chair and grinned. "Tyler heard from Sutton's lawyer. He's changing his plea."

"Really?"

"There'll be a hearing in about a week. They're negotiating the plea deal as we speak."

"Hard time?"

"Tyler is offering ten years. Figures they'll end up at three to four."

"Congratulations."

"I think the blackmail money rumor finally pushed Sutton over the edge, so thanks for that."

"Glad I could help. One more week, and you'll be able to sweep the blackmail under the rug."

"Finally. And no one found out. Not any of my donors. Not even my campaign manager. In the end, I caught all the breaks."

"Yes, you did. Keep your pants on until after the election."

"Don't you worry about that."


THE NEXT MORNING, shortly before 9:00 a.m., Jodi stood with a rental agent, a plump, middle-age woman in a red jacket and black slacks, on the front steps of a brick rental house with a two-car garage on an access road near a strip mall.

"This is a quiet neighborhood," the woman said, "families with young kids. No college students and no foolishness."

"It's exactly what I'm looking for."

"How many people will live here?"

"Just me."

"No husband? No boyfriend?"

She shook her head. "And no kids. I work from home."

The rental agent opened the door. "Like I said on the phone, it's a furnished rental. Nothing's perfect, but it's in good condition."

The living room contained two sofas and a TV. One bedroom was empty, the other contained a king-size bed, two side tables, a dresser, and a walk-in closet. A wooden table with four chairs filled the eat-in kitchen. The backyard was open to the neighbor's yard.

"I'll take it," Jodi said.

The rental agent opened her laptop on the kitchen table. "Great. Let's fill in the paperwork."

Jodi took out her new fake ID and provided the banking information that matched it. The rental agent filled in the lease and used her internet connection to check Jodi's credit score. All good.

Jodi smiled. "Can I pay the security deposit and the rent with cash?"

"Of course."

After they were done, the rental agent drove away, and Jodi drove the Honda CR-V into the garage. She opened the trunk, took out two suitcases and three bags of groceries, and brought them into the house. She set a fifth of whiskey on the kitchen counter. She did one last walk-through, making sure all the windows were latched and the front and back doors were locked. Everything was ready. She wouldn't come back here until after the jailbreak. She looked at her watch. Eleven-thirty.

She drove away from the new safehouse and circled around the neighborhood of duplexes and small, one-story houses to get a feel for the best way to lose a tail or to get to a major thoroughfare in a hurry. It was 12:30 p.m. by the time she got to the diner where she was meeting Gwen for lunch.

Big Momma's Tacos and More was a block west of the college campus. Jodi parked in the gravel parking lot and took a moment to focus herself. She didn't know why Gwen wanted to meet. She just knew it wasn't to catch up. And if Little Pap wanted her to go on another job—well, she was going to have to find an excuse that would stick. She took a deep breath, got out of her car, and went in the restaurant via the side door. Square-top tables filled the room. At the far wall from the main doors, several college students stood in line to order food at the counter. Gwen, dressed in yoga pants and an open flannel shirt over a green T-shirt, was already sitting at a table. She waved. Jodi went over to the table.

"I already ordered for you," Gwen said. "The special tacos and an iced tea. Hope you don't mind."

"Not at all." Jodi pulled out the chair cattycorner to Gwen and sat down.

"How have you been?"

"Good. I've been good. It's been a while."

"Since that incident."

"If that's what you want to call it."

"I feel like things were awkward between us when I dropped you off, but I didn't know what to say."

An unshaven guy in a T-shirt and jeans, a Big Momma's Tacos ball cap backward on his head, brought their food to their table.

"Looks good," Jodi said.

"The tacos are the best thing on the menu." Gwen sipped her iced tea. "Anyway, I just wanted to make sure we were still friends."

Jodi nodded. When were they friends? "Did you ask Little Pap about what happened?"

"Yes."

"What did he say?"

"That he had our backs. That Osborne's crew would have had to give us up."

"Do you believe that?"

"I do."

"Then there's nothing else to say about it." Jodi took a bite of a taco.

"You think that's stupid."

"Let's put it this way. I wouldn't go on another job for Little Pap without my own gun and my own escape route."

"You don't know him."

"Very true."

"How's your husband doing?"

"He's doing okay, given the circumstance."

"How are you set for money? We could organize a little job on the side."

"We had some money put back, so I'm still doing okay. Thanks for the offer." Jodi took the lemon slice off the rim of her glass and dropped it into her tea. "Have you ever thought of making a change? Going out on your own or trying something new?"

"Oh, sometimes I'm pissed off at Pap, but I don't want to be the boss. And I don't want to go back to school, so a straight job is off the table."

"What are you going to do when you can't be Little Pap's girl or one of his crew?"

"Become a bartender, I guess."

"So you do have a plan."

"If that's what you want to call it." Gwen sipped her tea. "What about you? What are you going to do if your man ends up in prison?"

"I don't know. I haven't thought about it." Jodi smiled. "Maybe I'm overconfident."

"Maybe you won't have to decide."

"Maybe I won't."

When they stood up after they finished lunch, Gwen hugged her. Then she left through the front door, and Jodi went back out the side door to the parking lot. Gwen was trying way too hard to create a sense of intimacy. They'd never been friends, not by any stretch of the imagination. They were barely acquaintances. So what was she up to? Must be related to why they searched her house. They were looking for something—something valuable. That was Little Pap's way. Well, Gwen was out of luck, because Jodi didn't have any tells, at least none obvious enough for Gwen to spot. But did Gwen really have a job teed up if she'd said *yes* instead of *no*, or was it a bluff? Guess she'd never know. She got into her car and headed back to the ranch house on Fish Creek Road. Now all she could do was wait until Lopez was finished installing the computer override.

GWEN DROVE out to The Three Little Pigs, where she found Little Pap in the back room, sitting on the sofa playing a video game. He turned off the TV when she entered the room.

"So?" he asked.

"She doesn't know that we broke into her house."

"How do you know?"

"She's got this big sister vibe. Wants me to change my life. She couldn't sell that if she didn't believe it."

"But she still might have the blackmail money."

"I don't think so."

"You two going on a job?"

"No. She said she had some money put back."

"And you believed her?"

"I believe her."

"Maybe the blackmail money story is all bullshit, or maybe she's a better liar than you think. It's worth one more try. We'll wait another week and then we'll search the house again."

FOUR DAYS LATER, just after the school bus made its afternoon run past the ranch house, Jodi got a phone call from Lopez. "You're all set."

"Meet me at the Stop & Go where we first met."

When Jodi got to the Stop & Go, Lopez's pickup truck was parked at the far end of the building. Three cars were at the gas pumps, and two cars were parked in front of the entrance to the building. She pulled in beside him and got out of her Honda with a manila envelope. She scanned the area to make sure no one was watching her before she went over to the driver's side of Lopez's truck. Lopez lowered his window.

"Have you got my money?"

"It really works?"

"You engage the override, and you can operate the van like a remote-control car as long as you're within range. The farther away you are, the more likely you're going to have weak signal problems or interference from objects between you and the van."

Jodi handed the envelope through the window. "Three thousand dollars."

He passed her the remote control. "I hope I never see you again." Lopez backed out of his space and drove off.

The next morning, Jodi parallel parked in front of a warehouse across the street from the county motor pool parking lot. She was wearing a gray wig and black-framed sunglasses with a sweatshirt and yoga pants. She crossed the street to the chain-link fence surrounding the motor pool and walked along the fence until she saw the prisoner transportation van. It was in an interior parking space on the other side of the nearest drive lane. She took the computer override controller out of her handbag and turned it on. The touch screen lit up. She tapped the icon to turn on the van. The van's engine started. She tapped the icon for the headlights. The headlights came on. She smiled. She put the van in reverse and backed it a few feet out of its space. Beautiful. She put the van into drive, moved it back into its space, and turned it off. Then she went back to the Honda.

Just like clockwork, the deputies pulled up in a sheriff's department cruiser, walked into the motor pool parking lot, and drove out in the prisoner transportation van. Jodi followed them to the county jail, where they parked at the loading dock. Jodi pulled off onto the shoulder of the road about a hundred yards farther down and adjusted her rearview mirror so that she had a clear view of the van. After the deputies went into the jail, Jodi turned on the remote again, holding it up to the window. She pressed on the starter icon. Nothing happened. She backed her car up about ten yards and tried the starter again. Still nothing. She backed up another ten yards and pressed the starter icon. The van started. She put it into reverse and backed it up a few feet. So she had about an eighty yard range to work with. That should be doable. Between the dart gun and the computer override, she should be able to handle the ambush on her own.

She drove back to the ranch house and called Betty Ricardo. "Betty, this is Jody Sutton."

"Jody, what can I do for you?"

"When is the hearing?"

"The day after tomorrow."

"First thing?"

"At nine-thirty. They'll drive him to the courthouse. If you want to see him, right before the hearing would be your best opportunity."

"Thanks. I'll see you there."

## 8

Two days later, at 8:00 a.m., Jodi sat in a stolen Honda Pilot on the side of the road across from the county jail, where she had a good view of the prisoner transport van. She was wearing throwaway gloves, sunglasses, and a floppy hat.

Randy and two other prisoners shuffled out of the building and into the van. They were all wearing orange jumpsuits, and their wrists and ankles were shackled together. It was the usual run to the courthouse. Jodi knew every turn and crossroad. She let the van get well ahead of her before she started to follow. She had plenty of time. There were two places on the way to the courthouse that were suitable to her plan. The best spot was a grove of oak and hickory trees about two miles before the city limits, and the backup spot was an abandoned gas station next to the railroad tracks about eight blocks into town.

After the first crossroad, she sped up to pass the prisoner transport van, raced ahead, and pulled onto the gravel shoulder in the grove of oaks and hickories about twenty feet before a massive oak located off the left shoulder of the road. As the van approached, she turned on the remote controller to the van's computer override, increased the van's speed and turned it left. Nothing happened. She pushed down harder on the controller button. Nothing. The van was almost to her when it finally lurched left across the oncoming lane, the brakes screeching as the driver tried to stop. The van plowed into the oak, crushing its front end. The airbags exploded. Jodi opened the liftback of the Pilot, took out a set of bolt cutters and the tranquilizer dart pistol, and trotted over to the wreck. The two deputies in the front were knocked out, their airbags hissing as they deflated. Jodi picked the lock on the side door on the van. Randy was rubbing his face.

"Jesus, that was your plan? I almost broke my nose."

"But you didn't."

She tucked the dart pistol into her jacket pocket and cut through the chains on Randy's handcuffs and ankle shackles with the bolt cutters. The other two prisoners, a fat, bald guy with a skull tattoo on his neck and a short Latino with a tiny beard, looked at her expectantly.

"Just hand them here," the bald guy said.

She glanced at Randy. He nodded. She passed the bolt cutters to the bald guy. The deputies started to stir. "Time to go," she said.

She and Randy climbed out of the van. The deputy in the driver's seat was shaking his head and turning to look into the back of the van. Jodi pulled out her dart gun, but the bald guy snatched the shotgun from the rack beside the deputy in the front passenger's seat, pumped it, and shot the deputy seated in the driver's seat. Then he pumped it again and shot the deputy in the passenger's seat.

"What the fuck did you do that for?" the Latino asked.

"Because I could."

The fat guy got out of the van right behind the Latino and pointed the shotgun at Randy and Jodi. "Drop the dart gun and give me the car keys."

"No," Randy shook his head. "It's three on one. You shoot one of us, the other two are going to swarm you."

"One of you will still be dead."

"And so will you."

"No keys," Jodi said. "It's stolen."

"I'm still taking it." The fat man backed across the road, keeping the shotgun pointed at Randy, Jodi, and the Latino, and then turned and ran toward the Honda after he reached the shoulder on the other side.

The Latino looked from Randy to Jodi. "Aren't we going to stop him? We need that ride."

Randy smiled. "That wasn't our ride out of here. That was our diversion." They watched the fat man drive away. "You're Hernandez, aren't you?"

"Yes."

"You better come with us."

"We need to get moving," Jodi said. "They'll expect the van at the courthouse in ten minutes."

They jogged through the woods to a one-lane dirt track at the edge of a farm field where a Ford Expedition was waiting. Jodi used the fob to open the back. The black duffels of weapons, a shovel, a toolbox, and two plastic shopping bags sat in the back. She flipped open the top on the toolbox and fished around in the loose tools for a moment. "Here we are." She handed Randy a handcuff key.

Randy unlocked his handcuffs and the loose ends of the cut ankle shackles and handed the key to Hernandez. Jodi pitched a shopping bag to Randy. He stripped off his orange jumpsuit and gym shoes and put on jeans, a golf shirt, and moccasins. Jodi tossed the other shopping bag to Hernandez. "Might be a little big."

"You two were prepared."

"Not getting caught," Randy replied.

While Hernandez changed clothes, Randy dug a hole at the edge of the field and covered up the shackles and the jumpsuits.

"Where are you going?" Hernandez asked.

"Can't tell you that," Randy said. "But we can give you a lift into town."

"I don't have any money or any friends here."

Jodi reached into her pocket, pulled out a wad of cash, and peeled off a hundred dollars in twenties.

"You'd just give me a hundred dollars?"

"The longer you're on the run, the better it is for us."

"I wouldn't give you up."

"Please, my friend," Randy said. "If you get caught, it's the only bargaining chip you have."

They got into the Expedition. Jodi backed down the dirt track to a turnaround spot and then drove out to a rural highway two miles west of the wrecked van. "Where to, buddy?"

"Have you got a car jimmy?"

"There's one in the toolbox."

"Can you give it to me and drop me off down at the college campus?"

She nodded. "We can do that. Stay down in the seat in the meantime."

After they left Hernandez on a street corner by a parking lot on campus, they drove back to the new safehouse, Randy lying down in the seat until Jodi had pulled into the garage and lowered the garage door. By the door to the kitchen, Randy pulled her into his arms. "You were doing your best work today," he whispered.

"Just missing my baby." She kissed him.

"Have I ever told you how lucky I am to be partnered up with you?"

"Not recently."

"Relentless. Unstoppable. You never flinch."

"Stop it."

"How safe are we here?"

"Safe." She kissed him again.

"We'll need to change cars again."

"We've got time."

"Then why don't you show me the bedroom?"

Afterward, standing in the shower with the hot water beating down on them, Jodi caught Randy up on her activities.

"So Little Pap's been acting as expected," Randy said.

"There's nothing surprising about him."

"True. But you know how he's getting his product into the jail."

"Just got lucky," Jodi replied.

"You make your luck, honey." He took her face in his hands and kissed her.

"It's good to have you home, baby."

"It's good to be home."

They finished showering. Randy went into the bedroom to get dressed. "Glad to be wearing my own clothes."

Jodi stood in the bathroom, putting on lotion. "Glad you got the prison smell off you."

"That bad?"

"Uh-huh."

Randy came back into the bathroom, combed his hair, and kissed her cheek. "It's almost eleven o'clock. I'm going to look on the TV and the internet for any top-of-the-hour reports on the breakout."

Jodi followed him into the bedroom and started getting dressed. "I'm going to make some coffee. Want some?"

"That would be great."

He went down the hall to the living room, sat down of the sofa, and clicked through the local TV channels, but there was nothing about the breakout. "Where's your laptop, honey?"

"On the dresser."

He went back to the bedroom, picked up the laptop, and carried it back to the sofa. On the internet, the story had already been updated several times. The two deputies found shot dead at the scene were both family men with young children. One escaped convict had been cornered while robbing a convenience store. Two employees were being held hostage.

Jodi came into the living room carrying two cups of coffee. "Anything?"

"The fat asshole is hunkered down in a Circle K, tying up police resources, which should give Hernandez a little more time to get out of town."

She handed him his coffee.

"Thanks."

"Maybe the cops won't catch up with Hernandez for a week or two."

"We could only be so lucky," Randy said. "Once we get rid of the Expedition, get some sort of vanilla ride. Then we'll wait things out for a few weeks, let the cops get back to their routine."

"We've still got the Escalade out in the storage garage."

"We have to leave it there. Too many people know it."

"I hate to bring this up since you just got out, but we're almost broke."

"What have we got left?"

"A little less than seven thousand dollars."

"That's not much."

"As soon as the FBI finds out you've escaped, they're going to be back on this case."

He nodded. "We need to stay off their radar, and we need to earn a pile of quick cash so we can disappear for a few months—maybe a year."

"We don't have time to start a new scam from scratch."

"No, we don't. And we don't have the cash to bankroll it. Have you got any ideas?"

"What about Kennedy's safe?" Jodi asked. "We know his building, and we owe him for trying to sell us to the Orange Hill Cartel."

"That would be tough. Kennedy's a putz, but we barely escaped the cartel the last time."

"Why would they still be around?"

"We disrupted their diamond smuggling. Kennedy's a gem wholesaler, so they might be using him."

"So you're saying *no*?"

"That's not what I'm saying," Randy replied. "In a lot of ways, it's a good idea. Chicago is far enough away from here to give us some breathing room. We already know Kennedy's building and cracking his safe wouldn't be a problem, but we'll need his fingerprint, and if he sees either of us, we won't be able to get it. So that means we need a partner."

Jodi chuckled. "What about using Chrissie to get his print? She been complaining about needing money. And we know she knows how to manipulate men."

"You just can't resist adding to the degree of difficulty, can you? She probably double-crossed us on the Brighton job, and her trying to reconnect with us is just what she'd be doing if she was working for the police."

"But we don't know for a fact that she double-crossed us, do we? And we don't have time to find another partner. We need to move on Kennedy as soon as possible. If we use her, the job goes quicker, which also means our risk from the Orange Hill Cartel is lower."

Randy stood up from the sofa and stretched. "Okay, so we use Chrissie to get Kennedy's fingerprint. She's an escort, so she's not going to be shy about doing whatever it takes. If she comes on board."

"She'll come on board."

"The trick is that we need to keep her on the outside while making her think she's on the inside. She can't sell what she doesn't know."

"And after the job is done, if it turns out she's working with the police, we deal with her then," Jodi said.

"Agreed. Let's work out the details."

MEANWHILE, Smith stepped into Brighton's office at the county administrative building. Brighton looked up from his laptop computer. "Shut the door."

Smith closed the door and sat down in the office chair facing the desk. "What have you heard?"

"Jailbreak. Dead deputies. Sutton was one of the prisoners."

Smith nodded. "It's a clusterfuck. The transport van crashed on the way to the courthouse."

"Anything wrong with the van?"

"Don't know yet. Three prisoners, including Sutton, escaped. One made it as far as the Circle K on Clayton Street. He'll be dead or in custody within the hour."

"What about Sutton and the other guy?" Brighton asked.

"No leads. The sheriff is hoping they'll turn up on a surveillance camera somewhere. They've got to buy gas, eat food, sleep somewhere."

"What about Sutton's wife?"

"She's missing, too," Smith said.

"So she's involved."

"Probably. Cheer up. This is good news for you."

"How so?"

"Now no one cares why you were being blackmailed. We've got two murdered deputies."

"Sad but true," Brighton replied. "Sutton is looking at murder or accessory to murder."

"Looks like you're a shoo-in for reelection."

"It would be a shame if Sutton died resisting arrest. Weren't you using Chrissie to get in touch with the wife?"

Smith nodded.

"Maybe she still has a good phone number."


LITTLE PAP, Jerry Jeff, and Gwen were sitting around the coffee table in the backroom at The Three Little Pigs. "Where did you get your information?"

"Our guy at the jail called me," Jerry Jeff replied.

"But there's nothing on the TV," Gwen said.

"It's all over the internet. Wrecked van. Dead deputies. Three escaped prisoners."

"So we're fucked," Little Pap said. "She was planning the jailbreak the whole time she was acting like she needed our help."

"You think they actually have the blackmail money?" Gwen asked.

"I don't know. But the only way to make money off them now is to sell them to the sheriff."

"We're not snitches," Jerry Jeff said.

"It's not snitching. They lied to us all along. Put our plans at risk. The sheriff is going to be watching anyone in the jail who was friendly with Sutton. So our drug business is going to have to stop for a bit. Sutton jammed us up, so we're going to jam him up. Do we know where they went?"

"They didn't go to that house on Fish Creek Road," Jerry Jeff said. "We've got guys watching it."

Gwen shook her head. "No clue."

"You were supposed to be working her," Little Pap said. "Looks like she was working you."

"I think I could have won her over if the robbery at Osborne's hadn't gone bad."

"Maybe." Little Pap turned to Jerry Jeff. "I want all our guys scouring the city, looking for the Suttons. If they haven't left town, I want them found. They're still worth a payday."

THE NEXT NIGHT at 11:00 p.m., as Chrissie was returning home from a waitressing shift, Agent Smith got out of his Ford Explorer and met her on the sidewalk in front of her house.

She took a step back. "What are you doing here?"

"Randy Sutton escaped."

"I heard about that. Not my problem. I did my part."

"Did you? Or were you working both sides of the fence?"

"That's not fair. I did everything you asked."

"I decide what's fair. We never found the wife."

"And that's why he escaped."

"Maybe you helped her evade capture."

"As I told you before, she dropped me off. I don't know where she went. I never saw her again. That's the truth."

"That's not much help."

"It's all I've got."

"You can do better than that. You're going to help me capture them."

"No."

"Or I'm going to arrest you for being an accomplice."

She folded her arms. "And I'll tell everyone about my relationship with Terry."

"No you won't. You won't expose yourself."

"Why not?"

"For all the same reasons that made it look like you couldn't be involved in the blackmail. It would ruin your reputation. Make it difficult to get a professional job. Make it hard to find a serious relationship."

"I don't know anything. What can I do?"

"Can you get in touch with them?"

"No. I don't know. Maybe. I've got the old phone number I used before, but that's all."

"I don't care how you do it. You get in touch with them. Tell them a sob story. Win them over. Find out where they are. Do that and you're in the clear."

"Five hundred dollars."

"Are you crazy? You didn't earn the five hundred I already gave you."

"Yes I did. I've got bills to pay. You and Terry are keeping me from escorting. You want me to work for you, you've got to pay me for my time."

Smith pulled a wad of hundred-dollar bills out of his pocket and counted out five. "I expect results."

"I'll do my best."

Agent Smith got back in his Explorer and drove away. Chrissie walked up the sidewalk to her front door and let herself in. The blackmail scheme had been too good to be true. She shouldn't have been greedy. She should have said no. Now she was in this mess up to her neck. They only ray of sunshine was the money Smith was paying her. She started down the hall to the bathroom. She hadn't deleted Jodi's phone number in her address book, but she had no idea if it was still good. And even if it was, what sort of lie could she tell the Suttons that would cause them to tell her where they were?

The next morning, Chrissie lay in bed, staring at the ceiling. She'd been tossing and turning most of the night, unable to sort through just how she was going to get out from under the FBI and get her old life back. And after she'd finally fallen asleep, her dreams involved missing car keys or house keys or not being able to find the classroom where she was supposed to take her final exam. She yawned and blinked and stretched her arms overhead. Did she have to get up?

Her phone rang. She rolled over, picked up her phone of the night table, and looked at the screen. Her mom. She scooted up to sit against the headboard and answered it.

"Hey, Mom."

"Christina." Her mom's accent seemed thicker than usual. "I haven't heard from you in a long time. I thought you were in an accident."

"No, Mom. I'm fine."

"Where are you?"

"I'm at college, Mom."

"Still at college?"

"It's only my junior year."

"Oh."

"How are you, Mom?"

"They're keeping me here. Won't let me leave. Whenever I try to go out the front door, they bring me back to this room.

"You're at the care center, Mom. You have trouble remembering things."

"Nonsense. I need to go home and water the plants."

"You live at the care center now. You sold your house."

"I don't believe you. Why would I do that? Who are you, anyway?"

"I'm your daughter, Christina."

"Stop lying. What do you want? Why did you call me?"

"You called me, Mom."

"You're not Christina. If you were Christina, you'd come visit me."

"I'll come to see you at Thanksgiving."

"Why?"

"I love you, Mom."

"Stop calling me *Mom*." Her mom ended the call.

Chrissie set her phone down and got out of bed. Her mom wasn't getting any better. The cognitive exercises weren't helping at all.

Chrissie pulled on her robe, made coffee, and brushed her teeth. Melanie and Bruce were already gone. She sat down in the kitchen with her coffee and took out her phone. There was no reason to put off making this call. She input the phone number she had for Jodi. It rang four times and rolled over to voice mail. "This is Chrissie Makarova. We need to talk. Please call me back."

She got up and got dressed for the day, but her phone didn't ring. Then she checked her backpack to make sure she was carrying the right books for her classes that day and started for the college campus. By the time she was walking back home that afternoon, she was no longer expecting a return call from Jodi. She looked through the scrap paper on her desk and in her desk drawers, just in case she had another phone number for Jodi or Randy, but she didn't find one. That evening, after dinner, she called the phone number a second time. It rolled over to voice mail again. She left a message. "It's Chrissie. I'm desperate. Please call."

## 9

The next morning, as Chrissie was walking between classes on campus, she received a call from Jodi.

"Sorry to be slow getting back to you, but we've been busy."

"You guys doing okay?"

"Always."

Chrissie stepped off the sidewalk and sat down on a short wall surrounding a raised flower bed. "I thought maybe now, with the breakout, you might need my help. Have you got anything going on? Anything at all? I could really use the money."

"We do feel bad about the last job falling through, and we are working on something. We'll get back to you in a few days."

"Nothing sooner?"

"Sorry. I'll be in touch. I promise. And I'm tossing this phone, so the next call will be from a new number."

"I'll be waiting."

Chrissie called Agent Smith and filled him in.

"A couple more days?"

"That's what she said."

"Let me know just as soon as you hear anything."

"I will."

She ended the call. She really hadn't accomplished anything yet, certainly not $500 worth. But in a few more days, Jodi would call her back. She'd find out what the Suttons were planning. She'd tell Agent Smith. She'd get him off her back, he'd capture the Suttons, and she'd be able to go back to her life.

On Friday afternoon, Chrissie was sitting in a Caffeination coffee shop, writing an essay for her eighteenth-century literature class on her laptop, when her phone rang. She didn't know the number, but she answered it anyway.

"Hey, Chrissie," Jodi said, "you still looking for work?"

"Yes."

"Come to Chicago."

"And do what?"

"We want you to get a man's fingerprints."

"Both hands?"

"Right hand index finger. How you do that is up to you. Sleep with him, don't sleep with him, we don't care. Just get the fingerprint."

"What are you going to do with it?"

"Come to Chicago and find out."

"What's the pay?"

"Three thousand dollars or twenty percent of the job after expenses."

"What's the job worth?"

"A lot more than three thousand dollars."

"How about you pay me ten thousand dollars?"

"We know we can pay you three thousand, no matter what happens. You want more than that, you have to share the risk."

"Okay."

"Okay what?"

"I need as much money as I can get, so I'll take one more chance with you."

"That's the spirit. I'll text you with a date and address in Chicago."

Jodi ended the call.

.  .  .

RANDY AND JODI were sitting on the sofa in their safehouse. Jodi set her burner phone down on the arm of the sofa.

"So she's in?"

"Yeah."

"Let's go over it one more time," Randy said. "Just in case we missed something. First, Chrissie. She made a deal with Smith and Brighton before."

"Looks that way, but if she did, we don't know how much she told them."

"True. But we know that she was willing to deal. Put herself ahead of the crew. That's the only explanation for her behavior that makes sense."

"So we can't trust her."

"And because she works as an escort, she thinks she's a lot better at manipulating people than she really is."

"Her clients want to be manipulated," Jodi said. "They want to believe in their fantasy relationship."

"So we only tell her what she needs to know, while making her believe that she's really our partner."

"This job should only take a couple of days. Get the fingerprint. Open the safe. The charade won't have to last long."

"And then we stiff Chrissie and put the sex video on the internet," Randy said.

"If she double-crosses us."

"What goes around, comes around."

"But we don't have to wait that long to deal with Little Pap."

"No. Last thing we do before we leave town is mail a packet to the investigative reporter at the *Putney Tribune*. The pictures you took of Jerry Jeff at the county motor pool and drugs being taken into the jail by a corrections officer ought to be the basis for a great series of articles."

"And let's not forget about Smith, Brighton, and the sheriff's department. Even if Chrissie isn't helping them, they're going to be looking for us."

"They're looking for us now. We've got to make money fast if we're going to disappear. That's why we're hitting Kennedy's safe and gambling on Chrissie to begin with."

CHRISSIE CLOSED her laptop and tossed her coffee cup into the trashcan on the way out the door of the Caffeination coffee shop. A cold front had pushed through overnight. Only a few customers huddled in their jackets were sitting outside, and she sat down at a table that was the farthest away from them and called Agent Smith.

"So they're in Chicago," he said.

"Don't know if they're there now. I know they'll be there to do the job."

"And she's going to text you the details?"

"Exactly. You'll know as soon as I know. And then I'm out."

"What are you talking about?"

"You'll know where they're at. You can scoop them up. Case closed. You don't need me for that."

"No, no, no. What if things don't go according to plan? What if they manage to slip away? You're the inside man. Our ace in the hole. You're going to Chicago, and you're going to stick with them until we have them in custody."

"I can't afford to miss class."

"How much class are you going to miss if you're in jail?"

"For what?"

"Looks to me like you're part of an ongoing conspiracy to aid an escaped murderer."

"That's crazy."

"We'll see what a judge has to say."

"So it's essential for me to go to Chicago?"

"Yes."

"That'll cost you a thousand dollars up front, plus another thousand when you arrest them."

"How long do you think you can keep bleeding me?"

"If you want my help, that's what I have to have."

"Okay. A thousand up front. Are you at home?"

"No."

"How quickly can you get there?"

"Thirty minutes."

"I'll drop by your house in an hour with the money."

"I'll be there."

Chrissie set her phone down on the table and held her head in her hands. What an asshole. The only conspiracy she was involved in was the one he'd put her in. She shoved her hands into her pockets. She needed to get Smith off her back so that she could get her life back to normal—classes, escort clients, hanging out with her friends. If going to Chicago and helping Jodi and Randy get their fingerprint would do that, then she had to do it. At least she was going to get $1,000 out of it, no matter what happened. That money would be in her pocket even if Randy and Jodi managed to slip away. And if Smith got them? Another $1,000. She just had to make sure that Randy and Jodi didn't figure out she was working for Smith. God knows what they would do to her if they found out.

She looked up as two women, college students by the look of them, came out the door of the Caffeination and onto the patio. But could she turn this situation into a bigger payday? The Suttons owed her $30,000 for the last job, even if it had fallen through. What if she stalled Smith until this new job was completed? She could keep all the money after Smith arrested the Suttons. How much would that be? Enough to pay next year's tuition? Enough to pay off her school loans? Enough to pay for all the extras at the care center until she had her first after-college job? That much money would certainly take the pressure off and let her focus on her grades next year.

But how dangerous would it be? Getting the fingerprint would be easy enough. But staying ahead of Jodi and Randy would be tough. They were professional liars and thieves. They would expect her to try to cheat them. But they weren't killers. If she kept up her guard, maybe she could fool them long enough to take the score. They were going to jail, either way. It was worth a try.

AN HOUR LATER, Smith pulled up in the driveway of Chrissie's house and parked behind the Jeep. Chrissie came out and climbed in the passenger's side of the Explorer. Smith handed her a wad of bills. "One thousand dollars."

"Thank you." She thumbed through it before she put the money in her jeans pocket.

He took a cell phone out of his jacket pocket and handed it to her. "I'll call you on this phone. Keep me in the loop."

"Okay."

"Text me with any new information before you leave for Chicago."

"Gotcha." Chrissie reached for the door handle but stopped. "What are you going to do if the Suttons find out I'm working for you?"

"They're not going to find out."

"If they do?"

"You run into trouble; you text me. I'll come running."

"Okay."

"You're doing the right thing."

She climbed out of the Explorer.

Smith backed down the driveway. When he first agreed to help Brighton, he was just doing a favor, paying back a favor, the usual sort of thing, one hand washing the other. But now he had a real chance to get out of this backwater and back into the game. Capturing the Suttons would be big news. Escaped fugitives wanted for murder. His old bosses would have to clear his record and bring him back to the Cincinnati office. He'd have a chance to do real police work again.

He stopped at the red light at the first intersection on campus. Class change was underway, students swarming across the street on the crosswalk. He called Brighton. His Explorer routed the call through its interior speakers.

"Terry."

"Tell me something good, Smitty."

"The Suttons are going to Chicago. I'm sending Chrissie with them."

"That's putting her in the deep end."

"She put herself there when she agreed to help with the blackmail."

"True enough. What's your plan?"

"I'm going to work with the Chicago field office to capture them."

"Why not turn it over to the US Marshals?"

"They'd have to start from scratch. I've got an informant in place."

"You want the credit."

"I do. I had to take the blame on that missing fentanyl, even though I had nothing to do with it. Bringing in the Suttons should even the score."

"This isn't going to draw attention to me, is it?"

"Absolutely not. Every step of the way makes the original blackmail less important. The Suttons'll definitely plead the murders out if they don't want life."

"Let me know if you need any help."

"You bet."

LITTLE PAP, Jerry Jeff, and Gwen were sitting at their table at the back of The Three Little Pigs. Happy hour was in full swing. The bar was crowded and most of the tables were occupied. The jukebox was rotating through country hits.

"We haven't found the Suttons anywhere," Jerry Jeff said.

Little Pap drummed his fingers on the table. "No grocery stores, no liquor stores, no real estate rental agents?"

"Nobody knows anything. They must have switched IDs."

"They're probably gone," Gwen added. "Between us and the cops, somebody would have found them."

Little Pap nodded. "You're probably right." He turned to Jerry Jeff. "Tell our guys to stop looking."

The waitress came by to see if they needed fresh drinks. Little Pap shook his head *no*. He watched her walk away before he spoke. "What about the jail?"

"Jamal's wife says that everything has settled down," Jerry Jeff said.

"Okay, let's try a delivery. Contact Lopez at the county garage and the prisoner transport deputies at the jail. Let's see if we can pass an empty package."

"You got it."


In CHICAGO, Jackson Kennedy, a skinny man whose beer belly bulged out of his gray suit jacket, sat in his private office in his building in the Prairie View Office Park. He was a jewelry wholesaler, the kind of man who carefully rode the line between legal and illegal activity, fencing the highest quality gemstones as well as buying and selling gemstones from around the world. Or at least that's what he had been until he tried to turn the Travelers over to the Orange Hill Cartel after they stole the cartel's diamonds, and he ended up under the cartel's thumb.

Kennedy turned off his computer, checked to make sure that the six-foot-tall safe standing against the wall was securely locked, and walked out into the open room in the front of the building, where Tim, a large, bearded man with a pistol holstered on his hip, sat at a desk watching the surveillance monitor as it switched among the cameras mounted all around the building.

"Come on," Kennedy said.

Tim followed him to the door, where he armed the security alarm before they walked out into the parking lot to Kennedy's Mercedes. Tim got behind the wheel. "Where to?"

"The apartment."

Tim drove to the Gardenia Apartments, next to a strip mall containing a Whole Foods Market and a UPS store. He pulled into the parking spot for apartment 210. "Need me?"

"Wait here."

While Kennedy was walking down the sidewalk to the apartment building, his phone rang. He looked at the screen on his smartphone. Mr. Wishes, his contact with the Orange Hill Cartel. He answered it.

"Hello?"

"Did our diamonds arrive?"

"Yesterday."

"Did you have a chance to examine them?"

"My appraiser's still looking at them, but they appear to be as advertised."

"Good. If there's a problem, call me. Otherwise, hold on to them for now."

"After my guy is done, I'll move them to the safe deposit box at the bank."

"Don't do that. I'll want to take them with me when I come, and that may be on short notice."

"I can't guarantee their safety if I don't put them in the bank vault."

"You'll guarantee whatever we say you'll guarantee." Mr. Wishes ended the call.

Kennedy put his phone back in his pocket. Asshole. That was all he needed. The Orange Hill Cartel throwing its weight around. He took the elevator up to the second floor. He wondered if he'd ever get the chance to get them off his back. Not now. Not today. Time to stop thinking about work. He unlocked the door to apartment 210 and opened it. A fortysomething redhead, all curves in her see-through nightie, was standing in front of him.

"You're a sight for sore eyes," he said. "How do you get more beautiful every time I see you?"

"Get in here, you. You're late. I have to leave in about an hour."

She pulled him into the apartment and started unbuttoning his shirt.

# 10

Two days later, Randy, Jodi, and Chrissie sat around a coffee table in an Embassy Suites motel suite in Chicago. Chrissie's wheeled duffel sat by the door to the suite.

"How was the trip?" Randy asked. "You fly or drive?"

"I drove," Chrissie said. "So now that I'm here, what's this job about?"

"There's a guy we know here who tried to cheat us," Randy began. "He's a jewelry wholesaler. We owe him some payback, and we need fast money, so we're going to crack his safe."

"Why do you need his fingerprint?" Chrissie asked.

"There's a fingerprint reader on the safe. So I can't crack it without his index fingerprint."

"But you're sure you can crack it if you have the fingerprint?"

"We've been in his office. We've seen the safe."

"Okay," Chrissie said. "So any way I can get it, you want the right hand index fingerprint."

"That's right," Randy replied.

"What about using the fingerprint from a glass?"

"That will do it."

"Then why do you need me? It's simple enough."

"Because he's met us before. So we can't take the print. And we need a player who can do what needs be done."

"Okay. So is he going to be an jerk if he finds out what I'm up to?"

"You might get smacked. But we'll be close enough to intervene if it all goes sideways."

"You up for this?" Jodi asked. "You can still say no."

"Just want to know what I'm in for," Chrissie replied. "I'll start by trying to collect the print in a public place. I brought all the clothes I'll need. Have you got a place for me to stay?"

"You're down the hall." Jodi handed her a room keycard.

"I want to shower and take a nap."

"Sure thing," Randy said. "Be ready at four thirty p.m. We're going to start tracking him from his offices."


CHRISSIE ROLLED her duffel down the hall to her room. Once inside, she set her duffel on the bed, opened it, took out her dresses and hung them in the closet. Then she kicked off her gym shoes, peeled off her leggings, and pulled her sweatshirt off over her head. She looked at her phone. Three o'clock. Time to call Agent Smith. She got out the burner phone and speed-dialed the number in the address book.

"Chrissie. News for me?"

"We're at an Embassy Suites."

"We know where you are. We're tracking your phone."

"Thanks a lot."

"Just keeping you safe. What's the job?"

"Robbing a jewelry wholesaler. I'll know more over the next couple of days."

"Keep your phone on at all times."

"When are you going to arrest them?"

"It'll take us a few days to set up."

"I can wrap them up for you. You can arrest them during the robbery. You'll get some great press."

"We'll see."

"Think about it."

"What's in it for you?"

"I just want to make sure that they never get out of prison."

"You keep in touch." He ended the call.

She set the burner phone on the night table, pulled off her underwear, went into the bathroom, and turned on the shower. Her plan was going to work if she moved fast enough. Get the fingerprint. Be there when Randy cracked the safe. Take the money just as the FBI pounced. Then escape with the cash while the FBI arrested Randy and Jodi. And do that without Smith realizing what she was up to. That would be the tricky part. She'd have to figure out a way as the time neared. But once she had the money, and Randy and Jodi were locked away where they couldn't come after her, it wouldn't matter if she still had the escort job. She'd be able to provide for her mom and finish school.

SMITH TURNED off the digital recorder that sat on the desk of Ulysses Cooper, the FBI special agent in charge of the Chicago field office, and scooted back in his chair. "There you have it. The Suttons are in town to rob a jewelry wholesaler."

Agent Cooper, a boyishly handsome man whose steel gray hair was combed back over his bald spot, looked Smith in the eye. "That's not going to happen."

"No, sir. We'll capture them before then."

Agent Cooper rocked back in his chair. "I've read your record. I know you were railroaded."

"Yes, sir."

"But that doesn't mean I should trust you. Why shouldn't I just take this case from you and send you home?"

"Because I've got this confidential informant already in place. She's going to keep us up to speed so that we'll be able to choose the best time and place to make the arrests."

"I want this all by the book."

"Yes, sir."

"No funny business. Every penny accounted for."

"Absolutely."

"At the first sign of trouble, I'll close you down."

"I'd expect you to."

Agent Cooper nodded his head. "You must want this pretty bad."

"Just want to prove I'm a good agent."

"When you get information, I get information."

"Yes, sir."

"And Smith, if this goes bad, I'm going to paint you with it."


At 4:30 p.m., Randy, Jodi, and Chrissie sat in a Nissan Sentra among the cars in the parking lot of the Winning Ways call center across the street from Kennedy's offices in the Prairie View Office Park. Kennedy's offices were in a tan, sheet-metal building with no outside signage. Across a grass strip to the south was a FedEx warehouse.

"Everything here is the same as when we were here last time," Randy said.

"I think the FedEx is new," Jodi said.

"You sure?"

"That parking lot wasn't here the last time. We had to hide the extra car on the other side of the call center."

Randy smiled. "The 4-Runner. What a beast. Glad it was there when we needed it."

"There he is," Jodi said.

Kennedy and a bearded man with a shaved head and a pistol holstered on his hip came out of the building. They got into a white Mercedes.

"Who is who?" Chrissie asked.

"Potbellied guy is Kennedy," Randy said. "The bearded guy must be the new bodyguard."

They followed the Mercedes across town to the Gardenia Apartments, where Kennedy went into the building. The bodyguard stayed in the car. About an hour later, Kennedy came out of the apartment building, and they followed the Mercedes into the near suburbs.

Traffic was stop and go until they turned off into a neighborhood of two-story houses with two-car garages. The bodyguard pulled up into the garage of a red brick house with a long front porch. Then he came out and got into a Jeep Cherokee parked on the street and drove away.

Randy parked on the street half a block down. Jodi checked the address on her laptop computer. "It's Kennedy's house. The owners are Jackson and Brenda Kennedy."

"Didn't know he was married," Randy said.

"What about the apartment?" Chrissie asked.

Jodi googled it. "It's a rental. No info at the property search website."

"But he's a player," Chrissie said. "He's got that look about him. Bet he was meeting his girlfriend."

"Probably so," Jodi said.

"Maybe that will be useful," Randy said.

They waited two hours. No one came out of the house, so they drove back to the Embassy Suites, stopping at a nearby steak house along the way. After they ordered their food, Randy turned to Chrissie. "On a job like this, the cops already after us, we prioritize safety. We never eat at the same place twice. We change cars and motels every few days."

"We want to move as fast as possible," Jodi added. "We need to make this score and disappear before the cops catch up to us. So that means a lot of boring surveillance work waiting for our opportunity to get Kennedy's fingerprint. Because once we have the print, we're golden."

"So it may seem like we're moving slow, but it's the fastest way," Randy said.

The next morning, they were watching Kennedy's house at 7:30 a.m. At 9:15 a.m., the bodyguard drove up in his Jeep, parked in front of the house, and walked up onto the porch to ring the doorbell. A few minutes later, he was backing out of the garage in the Mercedes, Kennedy in the passenger's seat.

They followed the Mercedes to Tony's 24-Hour Fitness Center.

Kennedy and the bodyguard went inside carrying gym bags. After they came out an hour and a half later, they drove out to Prairie View Office Park and went into Kennedy's building. At one o'clock, the bodyguard left the office and came back in a half hour with two white take-out bags. At 6:00 p.m., they drove back out to Kennedy's house and the bodyguard left. Randy, Jodi, and Chrissie waited for an hour before they went to dinner at an Italian restaurant.

"Work, gym, girlfriend—none of that helps us," Randy said.

"The gym might work," Chrissie said. "He has to drink something."

"You mean snatch his water bottle?" Jodi asked.

"If he has a reusable water bottle, we might pull the prints from that," Randy said, "but if he's buying a throwaway bottle, the recycle plastic is often too flimsy for the prints to be good."

"It's still worth a try," Chrissie replied.

Randy nodded. "True enough, which means you have to be ready to go into the gym."

Jodi googled Tony's 24-Hour Fitness on her phone. "You can get a trial membership online. You want me to set it up?"

"Go ahead," Randy said.

Jodi input Chrissie's information. "I'm forwarding the welcome email."

Chrissie looked on her phone. "I've got it."

The server brought their plates. After he left, Chrissie continued. "We could also try to get a print off the door handle on his car."

"Iffy at best," Randy replied. "Fingers are curled too much to get a clean print."

"What about going through the trashcan at his offices?"

"We don't want to end up on the surveillance footage."

"So other than the gym, where?"

"We're just going to have to keep shadowing him," Jodi said. "He's going to go to a restaurant or a bar sometime."

The next day, Kennedy went straight to work. The bodyguard went for take-out at noon. At 6:00 p.m. they left the offices and drove straight to Kennedy's house.

"This is going nowhere," Chrissie said.

"He's a business guy," Randy said, "so he's going to act like a business guy. We just don't know his pattern yet. Tomorrow or the next day he's going to go to the gym. Maybe he'll see his girlfriend on Thursday."

"Bet he'll be at happy hour on Friday," Jodi said. "Maybe take his wife out to dinner on Saturday."

Chrissie sighed. "So we've got to wait it out?"

"Patience is ninety percent of the game," Jodi replied.

The next morning, Kennedy and his bodyguard went to Tony's 24-Hour Fitness again. Randy, Jodi, and Chrissie waited in the parking lot for thirty minutes before Chrissie went in carrying her gym bag. She was wearing yoga pants and a hoodie with the hood up.

The woman at the counter, sports bra and bike shorts, checked her password and ID and made a photo of her for their database. "I can take you through the facility. Show you the equipment, the showers, and the pool."

"I'll be okay this time," Chrissie replied. "I'm in a hurry. I'm just going to get on an elliptical."

She walked back through the space toward the bikes, elliptical trainers, and treadmills. Off to her right she could see Kennedy and the bodyguard among several men who were using the benches in the free weight area. She stopped at the mat hanger, took down a mat, sat it down in an open area where she could watch Kennedy, and started stretching. Gym members were trickling in, getting on the equipment, providing her with more cover.

Kennedy was doing bench presses, his bodyguard spotting him. When he completed his set, he and the bodyguard added more plates to the bar, and the bodyguard did a set. Kennedy grabbed a water bottle from the ledge behind him, took a long pull, and put it back. When he was done, they moved the bench and reconfigured the weight bench rack to do squats.

Chrissie got up, went back to the front desk, and bought a bottle of water. Then she strolled back across the space to the elliptical trainers beyond the weight racks and benches. Kennedy's bottle was sitting there on the ledge behind Kennedy, and Kennedy and the bodyguard were facing away from it. A man to their left had just started a set of shoulder presses. On the other side of the weight benches were the entrances to the women's and men's changing rooms. Chrissie drank from her bottle, shouldered her gym bag, walked along the wall by the ledge behind the weight rack benches. When she came to Kennedy's water bottle, she set down her water bottle and picked up his, taking care to handle it from the top. Then she walked past the front desk and out of the building, holding the bottle down at her side.

When she got back to the car, Randy got out of the driver's side. "That's the bottle?"

"Yep."

He took it from her and held it up to the sky. "Maybe. Maybe the prints are good enough. Let me call my guy."

Randy dropped Jodi and Chrissie off at the Embassy Suites and then drove out to Suncrest Industrial Park to Meditec Fabrications, a custom prosthetic limb manufacturer. He parked in front of the white, sheet-metal building and pushed through the glass door into a small lobby, holding Kennedy's water bottle by the cap. A sign sitting on an old metal desk read *push the button for assistance.* Randy pushed the call button and waited. A young woman in a lab coat came through the swinging doors at the back of the lobby.

"Can I help you?"

"I'm here to see Frank. He's expecting me."

"I'll find him."

A few minutes later, a middle-age man in a lab coat, the fringe of hair on his bald head cropped close to his skull, came through the double doors and grinned. "It really is you. When was the last time I saw you?"

"I'm guessing three or four years ago."

"Still up to no good?"

Randy shrugged. "It's a living."

"Is that the bottle? Hand it here."

Frank held the bottle up to the overhead light and twirled it. "Is this the best you could get?"

"So far."

"Looks smudged. But maybe we can clean it up. How soon do you need the index finger? Yesterday?"

Randy nodded. "That would be nice."

"Expedited is going to cost you."

"Got to have it."

"Okay. I'll be in touch as soon as I know anything."

When Randy got back to their suite at the Embassy Suites, Jodi and Chrissie were waiting. "Well?" Jodi asked.

"He said *maybe*."

"So we still need to be looking for the next opportunity," Chrissie said.

"More like we're in a holding pattern," Randy replied. "But we also want to make sure we're ready to go. If the print is good, we could be cracking the safe tomorrow night."

"That soon?"

"That soon."

"We've got plenty of time," Jodi replied. "All we have to do is check our gear and pack up the room. And there's no reason to do any of that until we're sure the print's good. Let's go get some lunch."

After lunch, while they were sitting around the table in Randy and Jodi's room playing Spades, Randy's phone rang. It was Frank.

"What's the news?"

"We gave it a try, but we couldn't get a clean enough image off the prints on the bottle."

"Okay. We'll keep trying."

"I need a print with more definition and less smudge." Frank ended the call.

Randy looked at Jodi and Chrissie. "The print wasn't good enough."

"Are we going to make another try today?" Chrissie asked.

"We'll start fresh tomorrow," Randy said.

"Well then, if you guys don't mind," Chrissie said, "I think I'll go get some studying done."

"We'll give you a call when we're deciding where to go for dinner," Jodi said.

CHRISSIE WENT DOWN the hall to her room. Two days down. If they got the fingerprint tomorrow, got the prosthetic finger back the next day, it would be day three before they robbed the jeweler. Five days total. That was longer than she expected. Smith would be chomping at the bit. What could she say to him to slow him down? She got out her burner phone, sat on the side of her bed, and gave him a call.

"Well?"

"Things are taking a little longer than we planned. The safe has a fingerprint reader. Getting a good fingerprint from the jeweler is more complicated that we thought it would be."

"Back up a minute. What's the jeweler's name and address?"

"Jackson Kennedy. His offices are at the Prairie View Office Park."

"And you're trying to get his fingerprint?"

She explained what they'd done so far.

"Maybe I shouldn't wait. We could arrest all of you at your motel right now."

"Well, you're calling the shots, but you know how slippery the Suttons are. You guys come busting in, they might escape in the mayhem. Some innocent bystander might get shot. At the jeweler's, at night, there'll be nowhere for them to hide. And stopping a robbery in progress—that would make a great headline."

"Not if they escape."

"As long as I'm with them, you'll know exactly where they are.

"I'm not waiting forever. Two more days max."

"It might take three."

"Three, but that's it. If you aren't robbing the jeweler by then, we're taking you where you are."

"I'll push it along as fast as I can."

"And if a good opportunity to take them comes along before then, I'm not going to wait."

SMITH SAT in his Explorer across the street from the Embassy Suites. He looked up at the window of Chrissie's room on the third floor. He could call in FBI SWAT right now, shut down the elevators, and have SWAT teams go up the stairwells, clearing each floor until they reached the third floor and captured the Suttons. But if SWAT ended up in a gun battle with the Suttons, or they pulled the fire alarm and caused a general panic, Chrissie was right—they might escape in the confusion. The two of them mixed in with all the motel guests. There were too many opportunities for the Suttons to escape or innocent bystanders to be injured. Either of which would be a front-page news story, one that would keep him working in Putney, Ohio, or get him sent to an even more remote location.

He called Agent Cooper.

"I was wondering when I was going to hear from you. Why haven't you captured the Suttons?"

"I'm trying to avoid collateral damage. At a motel or a restaurant or even a highway stop, bystanders could get hurt. I want to catch them in the open where there's no chance of escape and a clear line of fire. Score a big win for the Bureau."

"Stop stalling. Taking them into custody is going to be tricky. Get it done."

"They won't escape, sir."

"Don't disappoint me."

"I won't."

Smith opened a map app on his phone, input Prairie View Office Park, and let the app guide him out to Kennedy's offices. He got in the left turn lane on the boulevard to turn onto Prairie View Avenue. There was a FedEx warehouse on his left. Then the avenue curved around past a strip of anonymous offices before it straightened out and ended at a cul-de-sac. To his right was the Winning Ways call center, its parking lot full of cars. To his left was Kennedy's offices. A sheet metal building with a large parking lot. No signage. As if he never did business here.

Smith turned around in the cul-de-sac and pulled over. It was a great place for an ambush. Hide a car in the call center parking lot, another down at that strip of offices, one more here in the cul-de-sac, out of sight. Once the Suttons were in Kennedy's building, they wouldn't be able to escape. They'd come out of the building with the gems. His team would swoop in from all sides. Fat headline in the *Chicago Tribune*. But no matter how good this trap was, he couldn't wait forever. Makarova needed to speed things up.

MEANWHILE, in Putney, Ohio, the sheriff, a highway patrol captain, and the investigative reporter for the *Putney Tribune* sat around a small table in the sheriff's office. The photos of Jerry Jeff and the corrupt deputies and a note explaining Little Pap's smuggling operation sat on the table in front of them.

"So someone mailed you these photos and the note?" the highway patrol captain asked.

The reporter, a dark-haired woman wearing a blue jacket and new jeans, nodded. "I spent a few days watching the county motor pool and the jail and saw the same pattern myself."

The captain continued. "Just out in the open?"

"Just out in the open," the reporter replied. "We're going with the story. I'm just giving the sheriff the heads up as a courtesy."

"So you can see my problem," the sheriff said to the captain.

The captain studied the photos. "No way this is bullshit? Photos fabricated somehow?"

The reporter shook her head. "They've been gone over by experts. And like I'm saying, I saw the same thing myself."

The captain pointed to Jerry Jeff. "And that's definitely Little Pap's man putting a package in the transport van?"

"Without a doubt," the sheriff replied.

"And those are two of your deputies taking a package out of the van and handing it to a corrections officer."

"Unfortunately."

"So you want my help?"

"I've got bad cops. I want to make sure I get all of them, but I don't know how many there are. And I don't want any information leaking out before we're ready to move."

The captain nodded. "Whatever you need."

The sheriff turned to the reporter. "Can you wait a week while we set up a sting?"

"What do I get?"

"The scoop. You'll be there at the takedown. You'll have full access."

"Let me check with my editor."

# 11

The next morning, back in Chicago, Kennedy went straight to work from his house. At 12:45 p.m. the bodyguard went for takeout. At 4:30 p.m., they left the offices and drove to Abracadabra, an upscale restaurant/bar at the end of a strip mall. Randy, Jodi, and Chrissie followed them in a Highlander.

The parking lot was mostly full, but Randy managed to squeeze into a spot with a good view of the front door. Jodi glanced into the back seat. "You're on."

Chrissie was digging through a bag of clothes. "Give me a second." She changed into a tight-fitting party dress that showed her cleavage and slipped on a button-up sweater. Randy turned in his seat to talk to her. "You're looking good. Check out the situation and give us a call."

Chrissie got out of the car. She was carrying a clutch purse in one hand. She pushed her way through the front doors, nodded at the woman standing at the hostess station, and walked to the bar in the center of the room. She sat on a stool on the left side. The bodyguard was standing at the end of the bar near the swinging door to the kitchen, nursing a beer. Kennedy was sitting at a table, talking with a gray-haired man dressed in a suit. He had an iPad open on the table, showing the screen to the man as he talked. They each had a glass of water and a glass of wine. The man took an occasional sip of wine. Kennedy was busy with his presentation.

The bartender came around to Chrissie's side. "How can I help you, Miss?"

"Vodka tonic, please."

"Could I see some ID?"

She handed him her driver's license. He examined it carefully. "You don't look twenty-one."

"I get that all the time."

He handed the driver's license back and turned to make her drink. Chrissie took her phone out of her purse and called Randy to fill him in.

"I'm going to sit tight, see if I get a chance," she said.

"If you need help, call."

Chrissie put away her phone and turned on her stool. Kennedy and the gray-haired man were standing. They shook hands. The man walked away. Kennedy sat down. A server approached him. They spoke.

The bartender set Chrissie's drink on the bar in front of her. As she picked it up, she noticed that Kennedy was watching her. Was he really being so obvious? She smiled and sipped her drink.

Kennedy stepped over to the bar. "I haven't seen you here before," he said. "And I know all the regulars."

"What makes you think I'm a regular?"

"I'm Jackson Kennedy," he said, sticking out his hand.

She shook it. "I'm Trish."

"No last name?"

"No last name."

He grinned. "Care to join me at my table?"

"Why?"

"Pass the time? Unless you're waiting for someone."

"I'm not waiting for anyone." She slid off her stool. "Let me pay for my drink."

Kennedy held up his hand to catch the attention of the bartender. "Jimbo, we're moving to my table."

The bartender nodded.

Chrissie sat in the seat where the gray-haired man had been sitting. She glanced at the end of the bar. The bodyguard was still there, watching but not watching. The server came back to the table with Kennedy's bill. "I've changed my mind," he said. "Could we get the cheese plate?"

"Yes, sir."

Chrissie watched as Kennedy picked up his wine glass with his right hand and took a drink, all his fingers and his thumb in contact with the glass. She sipped her vodka tonic. How to get the glass and get out of here?

"So what do you do, Trish?"

"I'm in school."

"What are you studying?"

"Hospitality."

He chuckled. "Really?"

"Really."

The cheese plate came. "Help yourself," he said. He picked up a slice of baguette, buttered it, and topped it with a slice of Swiss cheese.

She popped an olive into her mouth. "And what do you do, Jackson?"

"I'm a gem wholesaler."

"You're kidding me."

"No, it's not as glamourous as you might think. It's basically high-end sales to people who are in the business. So there's no fooling anyone." He finished his wine and flagged the server. "I'd like another glass of wine. The cab this time." He turned to Chrissie. "You want anything?"

"I'm fine."

The server took Kennedy's wine glass. Kennedy looked at Chrissie appraisingly. "Maybe I've got the wrong impression, so I'll approach this delicately. You being here at the bar, is that part of your hospitality work?"

"That depends on what you have in mind."

"That's something we'll have to discuss."

The server set the glass of Cabernet on Kennedy's right. Kennedy picked up the glass by the bowl and took a generous drink. His phone rang. He set down his wine and glanced at the screen. "I have to take this. I'll be right back." He got up and walked back toward the men's room.

Chrissie watched him walk away. One firm touch. As clean a set of prints as she was going to get. The bodyguard was watching Kennedy. Chrissie picked up Kennedy's wine glass by the stem, emptied it into the gray-haired man's glass, and then held the glass at an angle so that she could check for the fingerprints. They didn't seem to be too smudged. She stood up, wine glass held upside down at her side, and walked out of the bar.

As she stepped out into the parking lot, she felt a hand on her shoulder. The bodyguard was behind her. "Don't touch me."

"Where are you going?"

"I don't know you," Chrissie said. "Get away from me." Out of the corner of her eye, she saw Jodi rushing toward her.

Jodi took out her phone, opened the camera, and put it on video. She held her phone up. "I'm filming you, mister. I saw the whole thing. Stay away from her." She turned to Chrissie, still holding the phone up. "You okay, honey?"

"Thanks for your help. This guy just started following me."

The bodyguard held his hand up in front of his face, opened his mouth to speak, but instead turned and went back into the bar.

Chrissie held up the wine glass. "I've got the fingerprints."

"Let's get out of here," Jodi replied.

MEANWHILE, Kennedy was standing at the back of the restaurant talking to his wife on the phone.

"That's not how it is, Brenda. I'm here with a client."

"Then how can you talk to me?"

"He just left."

"So now it's just you and Tim?"

"Who else would it be?"

"How about the hairstylist you've been screwing?"

"I'm not screwing Rhonda. Why are you so jealous? She just cuts my hair, that's all."

"That's not what her husband thinks. He sent me a video of you going into your love nest."

"I don't know what you're talking about. I'm coming home right now. We've got to talk this through."

"You're not coming home. You come here and I'm calling the cops."

"Brenda, please."

"I'm putting a suitcase on the front steps."

"Give me a chance."

She ended the call.

Kennedy looked at the screen on his phone. He wanted to call Brenda back, but he knew that was the wrong move. What a mess. He was going to have to do a lot of groveling to win her back. It was going to be tricky, particularly if there really was a video, but he'd get it done. Brenda wouldn't hold out forever. If he worked it right, she'd be gaslighting herself by the end of the week. And Rhonda? Why had he let that get out of hand? He didn't even really enjoy the sex that much anymore, but there she was, offering herself. He just hadn't been able to turn it down. Well, all that was over now. He'd have to find a new haircutter. A man.

He looked back across the room to his table. The tasty bit was gone. What a shame. Now he was going to have to sleep alone. He glanced around. Where was Tim?

Then he saw Tim come through the front door. He went back to his table. Tim met him there.

"Where did you go?"

"The girl left. I thought it was suspicious. I followed her."

"And was it suspicious?"

"I don't know. It was weird."

"Sit down. We're going to eat dinner here. I'm in the doghouse with Brenda. She found out about Rhonda."

"Oops."

"You can say that again. I'm going to be sleeping at the office for a few days."


"GREAT JOB, CHRISSIE," Randy said. They were in the Highlander headed back toward the Embassy Suites, the evening traffic bumper to bumper.

"We should stop off for some dinner," Jodi said. "Where do you want to eat?"

"Let's let Chrissie decide," Randy said.

"I don't really care," Chrissie said. "Chinese would be nice."

"You eat family style?" Randy asked.

"Absolutely. I want a taste of everything."

"Okay, check your phone for a place that's on our way."

"Take a right at the light. John-Jo's Chinese and Thai is two blocks down."

Randy pulled into the parking lot and parked in the closest available space to the entry. Inside, the restaurant was decorated in Chinese kitsch, golden dragons on red paint, but the tables were covered in white tablecloths. Traditional music played in the background. The dining room was mostly full, but the hostess seated them immediately. After they ordered their food, Chrissie said, "So what's next?"

"Take the glass to my guy," Randy said. "If he can pull the prints, we're in business. Otherwise, we'll have to make another try."

"Can you do that tonight?"

He shook his head. "First thing in the morning."

"And I'm going to do some surveillance at the office park," Jodi said. "The safe is in Kennedy's office, so we need to know as much as we can about his security system and what's going on at the other offices."

"Then when we've got the prosthetic index finger, we'll go in and take Kennedy's money."

"Easy peasy," Jodi added.

"So it's a busy day tomorrow. Fingers crossed," Randy said.

"I can't wait," Chrissie replied.

EARLY THE NEXT MORNING, at the county motor pool in Putney, Ohio, an undercover state police operative took photos of Jerry Jeff putting a package into the prisoner transport van and waving to the deputies who came to drive the van to the jail. While Jerry Jeff was driving back to The Three Little Pigs, he was pulled over on a county road by a highway patrol cruiser. Two troopers climbed out of the cruiser, guns drawn, pulled Jerry Jeff from his truck, handcuffed him, read him his rights, and loaded him into the back of the cruiser.

When the deputies parked the transport van at the loading dock at the jail and took the package out and passed it to a corrections officer, they were swarmed by a tactical team and arrested. The sheriff opened the package in front of the highway patrol captain and the *Putney Tribune* reporter. It contained dozens of small baggies full of white powder, which proved to be heroin.

After Jerry Jeff was processed into the jail, he was given his phone call. Instead of calling a lawyer, he called Little Pap.

"Sit tight and keep your mouth shut," Little Pap said. "I'll take care of you."

LITTLE PAP WAS BANGING his landline handset on the edge of his desk when Gwen pushed through the doors into the back room. "What happened?"

"Jerry Jeff's been arrested. Our smuggling operation in the jail is blown."

"Did they catch him with the dope?"

"Don't know the details yet."

"Jerry Jeff was the guy. The deputies, the corrections officers, the prisoners, and their wives—Jerry Jeff was the only guy they knew." She stepped around the desk, stood behind Little Pap and put her hands on his shoulders. "As long as he doesn't talk, you're in the clear."

"No one can take the pressure of that much weight."

"What do you want to do?"

"Call Larry. Tell him to get down there, talk to Jerry Jeff, find out what the charge is, and get him out on bail.

Gwen got out her smartphone and looked in her contacts for McMurry Law Offices. "Jerry Jeff's not going to talk."

"Get Larry down there."


MEANWHILE, in Chicago, while Jodi and Chrissie were checking out of the Embassy Suites, Randy drove back out to Suncrest Office Park to Meditec Fabrications to meet with Frank. When Frank came through the double doors into the lobby, he didn't even say hello. He just pointed. "Is that the glass? Hand it here."

Frank took the wine glass by the stem and held it up to the overhead light and twirled it. "This one looks a little better."

"It's not smudged."

"I know. The touch is a little light, but I don't think that's a problem. You still want it expedited?"

"Got to have it ASAP."

"Okay. I'll be in touch as soon as it's done."


CHRISSIE WAS SITTING on the sofa in Randy and Jodi's suite in the Comfort Inn Suites when Randy got back from Meditec.

Jodi got up from her chair. "Well?"

Randy smiled. "Print is good. Frank's expediting our job."

She hugged him. "Finally. We're in business, baby."

"You sure?" Chrissie asked. "The prints are definitely good enough this time?"

Randy nodded. "Time to make the final preparations."

Chrissie stood up. "What do you need me to do?"

"You've done your part," Randy said. "We'll take care of the rest."

"You sure?"

"Nothing for you to do right now," Jodi said.

"Okay then, I'm going down to my room to pack my work clothes."

When Chrissie got into her room, she called Agent Smith. "We've got a good fingerprint. The prosthetic finger is being made right now."

"So when's the robbery?"

"As soon as we get the finger. Tomorrow or the next day I bet."

"Nothing firmer?"

"You'll know when I know. Be ready."


MEANWHILE, back in Randy and Jodi's suite, Randy looked out the window down at the half-full parking lot. A mom and dad and two middle schoolers were unloading a SUV. Nothing out of the ordinary. "Have you seen any cops?"

"No," Jodi replied. "No cops and nobody suspicious. Maybe we're out ahead of trouble for a change."

Randy turned back into the room. "Either we misjudged Chrissie, or she's in contact with Brighton or Smith."

Jodi shrugged. "She could have been sharing information before but not doing it now."

"That would be the smart move. I don't think she's that smart."

"What do you want to do?"

"We need to search her room."

"Might not be any evidence there."

"Yeah, but it's a place to start."

"When and how?"

"Let's rig up something after you get back from checking Kennedy's offices."

THAT AFTERNOON, Jodi went out to Prairie View Office Park, where she studied the exterior of Kennedy's building and the nearby office buildings, noting the surveillance cameras and alarm systems. The Winning Ways call center parking lot was full, ten cars were parked in the FedEx warehouse parking lot, and only three cars were parked at the strip of anonymous offices on Prairie View Avenue on the way to Kennedy's building. When she got back to the motel, she pulled up a GPS map of the area on her laptop.

"Three ways to get out of there," she said, pointing at the map. "The main entrance to the office park, the side entrance from the neighborhood, and a short hop over the grass to the FedEx parking lot and the street from there."

"What about the surveillance cameras?" Randy asked.

"Kennedy has five. One on his parking lot, one on his front door, one on each side, and one at the back, just like before."

"So he hasn't made any changes?"

"Doesn't look like it."

"There's still a blind spot at the back door?"

"Looks like it."

"So we could escape there, but it's no help getting in. Where do the phone lines and fiber optic cable come in?"

"Right side of the building."

"And that's covered by a camera?"

Jodi nodded.

"So how are you going to get into the building without being seen?" Chrissie asked.

"We aren't," Randy replied. "We're going to cut the fiber optics and the phone lines and erase the surveillance log once we're inside." He turned back to Jodi. "Do we have to worry about the surveillance cameras at the call center?"

"Too far away."

"So we're set. We cut the communication lines and go in through the front. Bypass the local alarm. Crack the safe." He turned to Chrissie. "You'd be better off waiting for us at the motel."

She shook her head. "I'm not leaving your side until after we divide up the money."

"That's your call. You're going to get your money, either way."

"I'm going."

"Suit yourself."

Jodi closed her laptop. "Is that everything?"

"Checking our gear and packing—no reason to do that until we have the prosthetic finger."

"So we're just killing time?"

"Yep."

"Hey, Chrissie," Jodi said, "want to come to the swimming pool with me?"

"I don't think so. I should probably study. I need to be caught up with my classes when I get home."

"Come on. Randy won't go to the pool, and I don't like to go by myself. An hour won't kill you."

"I don't know."

"It'll do you good to relax."

"Okay. Just an hour. I really do need to study. I'll go get my swimsuit on."

"I'll come down to your room after I change."

Chrissie left the room. Jodi went into the bedroom area and got her swimsuit out of her underwear drawer. She started undressing.

"So you're going swimming and I'm going fishing," Randy said.

"That's the idea," Jodi replied. "I'll text you as soon as we're getting on the elevator."

After Randy received Jodi's text, he went down the hall to Chrissie's room and picked the lock located under the keycard reader. Inside, textbooks were piled on the dresser, the clothes she'd been wearing were laid out on the king-size bed, and an open suitcase lay on the floor near the bathroom.

Randy knelt by the suitcase and carefully felt through the clothes.

Nothing incriminating. He opened the dresser drawers. The lower two were empty, the upper two held underwear and nightclothes. He went to the bed and checked the pockets of her pants. In her handbag, among the lipstick, loose money, and breath mints, he found a cheap cell phone. Not the smartphone he always saw her using. It wasn't password protected and there was one contact in it. No name, just a phone number. So she was dirty. He put the phone back where he found it.

Then he felt through the clothes in her closet and poked through her bathroom kit. There was nothing else of interest. He looked over the room one more time, making sure he hadn't disturbed anything, and left.

When Jodi got back from the swimming pool, Randy told her what he had found.

"Her playing it straight was just too good to be true," Jodi said.

Randy nodded. "But what I want to know is who she's reporting to. If it's the cops, why haven't they arrested us yet? We're fugitives."

"What about if Smith's running the show? What if he's helping Brighton somehow, or if he's got some personal reason for waiting?"

"Or maybe Chrissie is leading him on."

"Why?"

"Who knows?"

"We're not going to know what's really going on until it's too late," Jodi replied. "And we can't just run. We've got to have Kennedy's money."

"Nowhere else to pick up the cash we need. Waste of time robbing a bank, restaurant, or liquor store—nobody carries cash anymore. And we don't have enough money left to set up even the flimsiest score."

"Maybe we need an excuse to keep Chrissie from coming on the job."

"That would just make her suspicious. Then God knows what she would do. We're just going to have to be super careful."

· · ·

THE NEXT MORNING, Randy, Jodi, and Chrissie checked out of the Comfort Suites. While they were rolling their luggage out to their cars, Randy got a text from Frank at Meditec Fabrications. *Job completed.*

He stopped in the parking lot to respond. *On my way.*

"What's up?" Jodi asked.

"The finger is ready," Randy replied. "Chrissie, why don't you check us in at the Holiday Inn Express while we pick it up?"

"Why can't I come with you?"

"Because my guy is squirrely. He doesn't want to make any new friends."

"Okay. I'll meet you at the Holiday Inn Express."

They loaded all the luggage into the trunk of Chrissie's Honda. Then Randy and Jodi drove out to Meditec Fabrications. Jodi stayed in the car while he went inside. Frank was waiting in the lobby. He handed Randy a small plastic box. Randy removed the lid. A plastic index finger rested in a foam bed. "You sure this will work?"

"Our biometric scanner reads the fingerprint as human."

Randy took an envelope out of his jacket pocket and handed it to Frank, who opened the envelope and thumbed through the cash inside.

"We good?"

"Appreciate the business," Frank replied.

Randy handed the box to Jodi after he got back in the car. She opened it, took out the index finger, and rolled it over. "Looks like a real finger."

"Frank does excellent work."

"Kind of creepy." She put the finger back in the box. "This would be a good time to pick up the extra vehicle."

"Let's do it."

They drove out of the industrial park, passing an autobody shop and a landscape materials store before pulling into the parking lot for Bryce Custom Auto Paint. Several cars were parked around the side of the building. There was no surveillance camera. Jodi pulled over by a tan Camry with slight damage to the front left fender. "How about this one?"

"Works for me." Randy got out, pulled a specialty tablet computer out of his jacket, and used it to mimic the Camry's key fob, open the door, and start the engine. Jodi followed him out of the lot and across town to the FedEx warehouse adjacent to Kennedy's offices, where he parked in the corner of the lot farthest from the security cameras. He put a Glock in the glovebox before he got out and got back in the car with Jodi.

"That should do the trick," Jodi said.

"Belt and suspenders, baby. Belt and suspenders."

AFTER CHRISSIE CHECKED in at the Holiday Inn Express and Suites, she grabbed a rolling cart from the lobby and took their luggage up to their rooms. Then she went into her room, sat at the table by the window where she could watch the parking lot in front of the motel, got out her burner phone, and called Agent Smith.

"Yeah?"

"The job is going to be tonight."

"Are you sure? I don't want to waste resources staking out a place where nothing is happening."

"I'm pretty sure. They went to pick up the prosthetic finger with the fingerprint on it and we've moved motels. So I'm thinking overnight tonight. It can't be done during the day. Middle of the night is the only time the office is guaranteed to be empty."

"You've done a good job so far, Chrissie. Don't fuck it up."

"Trust me, Agent Smith, I want this over with even more than you do. Anything else?"

"No." Smith ended the call.

SMITH WAS SITTING in the parking lot of a Caffeination coffee shop around the corner from the Holiday Inn Express and Suites. He'd followed Chrissie instead of the Suttons because he was afraid they might spot him tailing them and he knew they were going to be reconnecting with Chrissie at the new motel. He set his phone down on the passenger's seat and sipped his latte. Finally. The waiting was over. They'd take the Suttons coming out of Kennedy's office. Empty parking lot, small likelihood of civilian injuries, and the added glory of stopping the robbery. He picked up his phone.

"Agent Cooper, tonight's the night."

"You've certainly taken your time."

"Wanted to do this right."

"Are you going to involve the local police?"

"No. Want to keep this simple."

"How many agents?"

"Three cars, six agents."

"I'll have the agents detailed to you."

"Thank you, sir."

AT 4:00 P.M., Smith stood at the front of a conference room in the FBI offices, a map of Prairie View Office Park on the screen behind him. The six agents that had been assigned to him were sitting around the table taking notes. Smith pointed out Kennedy's offices.

"The Suttons and my CI are going to break into this building to rob a safe. When they come out, we're going to take them." He pointed to the call center's parking lot across Prairie View Avenue. "I'm going to be waiting in this lot in an unmarked car. The lot is full all night, so I won't stand out. When they go into the building, I'll contact you. You move into position at these three spots." He pointed out the anonymous strip of offices, the call center, and the cul-de-sac. "From these locations we'll have eyes on the front and back of the building. When they exit the building, we snap our trap shut, and take them in the parking lot before they can escape or go back inside."

An agent raised his hand.

"Yes," Agent Smith said.

"What are they stealing?"

"Cash or gems. Maybe both."

Another agent chimed in. "But they're fugitives, aren't they? Why can't we take them now, before they commit another crime?"

"The Suttons have proven time and again that they can Houdini out of situations where they should have been caught. This setup should make that impossible." Smith looked around the room. "Anything else?" No other hands went up. "Get some rest. It's going to be a long night."

# 12

At 2:15 a.m., Randy, Jodi, and Chrissie sat in a stolen Dodge Dakota in the far corner of Kennedy's parking lot, waiting for the FedEx semitruck to finish unloading into the FedEx warehouse. At 2:24 a.m., the driver slammed the back doors to the trailer shut and rolled out of the parking lot.

Randy, Jodi, and Chrissie, all dressed in black, climbed out of the Dakota and made their way across the parking lot to Kennedy's building. Jodi moved off around the right side of the building to cut the phone and fiber optic lines, while Chrissie followed Randy to the front door, where he picked the deadbolt lock. Once inside, he pulled a small tablet computer from his duffel and plugged it into the burglar alarm keypad so that it could generate the passcode to disarm the alarm. Jodi came through the door just as Randy finished punching in the passcode.

AGENT SMITH, sitting in a Ford Taurus in the call center parking lot, watched them get out of the Dodge truck and break into the building. He got on his comms. "They're inside. Move into position."

Three black Explorers moved into place at the anonymous strip of offices, the call center, and the cul-de-sac. Each SUV responded in turn, "In place."

"Keep an eye out," Agent Smith replied. "I'm going in."

Smith climbed out of his unmarked car and crept across the street into Kennedy's dark parking lot, where he sidled up on the far side of the Dakota. The driver's side door was unlocked. He peered at the front of Kennedy's offices, but he couldn't see anything. He pressed his comms. "Any lights on in the building?"

One of the agents in the cul-de-sac replied, "Lights on in the back of the building."

Smith eased open the truck door. As soon as the interior light came on, he moved as quickly as possible to pull the hood latch and shut the door. Then he waited for a minute, watching the building. He pressed his comms again. "Any movement in the building?"

"Nothing has changed," the agent in the cul-de-sac said.

Smith snuck around to the front of the truck, lifted the hood, pulled a multi-tool from a sheath on his belt, opened the wire cutters, and cut one of the battery cables. Then he lowered the hood and scampered back to the Taurus. When he was back behind the wheel, he tapped his comms. "The truck is disabled."


RANDY, Jodi, and Chrissie moved quietly through the front area of Kennedy's offices, going straight down the hall to Kennedy's private office. Once they were inside, Randy shut the door and turned on the lights. They all looked at the six-foot-tall safe sitting against the left wall. Randy frowned. "It's different. Combination dial instead of a keypad. But it still uses the biometric pad."

"Is it the index fingerprint or are we screwed?" Jodi asked.

"Let me check." Randy took a small notebook from his duffel and looked up the brand of safe. Then he found the serial number on the side at the bottom of the safe and found it on the list. This one had a three-number combination paired with an index finger biometric pad. "We're good to go."

"How are you going to open it?" Chrissie asked.

"Stay out of his way and watch," Jodi replied. "There aren't very many people anymore who can do it old school."

"Just requires patience," Randy said.

He got out a piece of graph paper, spun the dial on the safe to reset the lock, and started cracking the safe, listening for the clicks that indicated the contact points in the locking mechanism, and graphing the results. Once he accounted for all three of the combination numbers, he had to determine their order. There were six possible combinations. He tried the first combination and placed the plastic index finger on the biometric scanner. Nothing. He tried the second combination. Nothing. But after he put in the third combination and placed the index finger on the biometric pad, he heard a sharp click. When he turned the handle, the bolt slid back into the door. He glanced back at Jodi and Chrissie and smiled. "*Voila.*"

He swung the door open. Banded bundles of cash were stacked in the bottom half of the safe, while the upper half contained trays labeled with the names of different kinds of gems. A folder lay on top of the cash. Jodi passed the folder to Randy, pulled a ripstop nylon bag out of the duffel, shook it open, and started putting the money inside.

"What's in the folder?" Chrissie asked.

"Bearer bonds," Randy replied.

"So we can cash them in?"

"I wish. They're a pain in the ass to deal with and have to be redeemed in person. We're leaving them."

"What about the jewels?" Chrissie asked.

"Gems have to fenced," Randy replied. "That's not a problem we need right now."

"So how much money is there?"

"I'd guess well over one hundred grand."

"Sure you want to leave the gems?" Chrissie asked.

"Won't be able to get rid of them for six months at least."

"Why?"

"Relax," Jodi added, "you're going to get at least twenty-five thousand dollars." She shoved the last bundle of cash into the bag and zipped it shut.

The door to the office swung open. Kennedy, dressed in pajamas, stepped into the room holding an AR-15 rifle to his shoulder in a two-handed firing stance.

"You two? I'll be damned. And the girl. On your knees. Any hands move toward pockets, I'm shooting."

Randy, Jodi, and Chrissie knelt.

"Now lay down with your hands stretched out in front over your heads."

They lay down. Kennedy came around behind them and kicked their legs apart. "That's better." He got out his smartphone and called Tim. "I need you now." He put his phone back in his pajama pants pocket.

"What are you going to do?" Chrissie asked.

"With you?" Kennedy replied. "I don't know. These two, I'm turning them over to the Orange Hill Cartel."

"That would be a mistake," Randy said.

"Shut up," Kennedy said.

"A real error of judgment."

Kennedy kicked Randy in the ribs. "I said shut up." Chrissie started whimpering.


TWENTY MINUTES LATER, the FBI agents on stakeout watched a Jeep Cherokee drive up to the front of Kennedy's offices. A large, bearded man got out and went into the building, moving as if he had every right to be there.

"Who was that?" One of the two agents in the Explorer in the call center parking lot asked over the comms.

"Doesn't matter," Agent Smith replied. "We'll figure out who's who after the Suttons are in custody."

"Why don't we move into the parking lot now?"

"If they see us, they won't come out of the building. We don't want them to have any cover when we swoop in. Stay alert."

Smith studied the front door. The jeep was parked too close to the building for him to risk disabling it. And the Suttons had been inside way too long. They should have already come out by now. Who was this extra player? It didn't matter. They still had the advantage. They just had to be ready to spring.

KENNEDY WAS STANDING OVER RANDY, Jodi, and Chrissie with the rifle trained on them when the lights came on in the outer office and Tim came into the back office.

"What took you so long?" Kennedy asked.

"Had to put my pants on," Tim replied. He looked down at Chrissie, Jodi, and Randy. "The honeypot. I knew something wasn't right about her. And the other woman was outside the bar. Must have been waiting for her."

"Search them and zip-tie their hands behind their backs. Start with him." Kennedy gestured toward Randy with the barrel of his rifle.

Tim patted Randy down, emptied his pockets, and zip-tied his wrists, taking care to stay out of Kennedy's line of fire. He put Randy's wallet, phone, and a snub-nosed revolver on the desk.

"Her next." Kennedy pointed to Jodi.

Tim patted her down, zip-tied her wrists, and put her smartphone and the truck fob on the desk next to Randy's wallet. Then he turned to Chrissie, emptied her pockets, and zip-tied her wrists.

Kennedy unzipped the ripstop nylon bag and looked at his money. "So you bastards were going to rob me."

Randy, Jodi, and Chrissie didn't answer.

Kennedy spoke to Tim. "What's in the duffel?"

Tim squatted to look inside. "Burglary tools, a notebook, another ripstop bag."

Kennedy kicked Randy in the head. "Not so smug now, are you?"

"What do you want to do with them?" Tim asked.

Kennedy kicked Randy again. "I'd like to kill him, fuck the women, and then sell them, but I can't. The Orange Hill Cartel wants them, so we're going to lock them in the storeroom. Then I'm going to call their guy."

Tim pulled them to their feet one at a time. He and Kennedy herded them down the hall, through another office, and into a storeroom that contained cleaning supplies and equipment.

"Hold the rifle." Kennedy handed the rifle to Tim, who kept it trained on Randy, Jodi, and Chrissie. Kennedy picked up the broom that was leaning against the wall by the shelves, grabbed it by the base of the handle near the brush, and wacked Randy across the back. Randy turned to the wall, trying to protect his face and ribs, but Kennedy beat him until he collapsed to the floor. Then Kennedy started on Jodi. Chrissie shrieked and got down in the corner with her head between her legs. In a few more minutes it was her turn. After they were all limp on the floor, Kennedy tossed the broom against the wall and locked them into the storeroom.

"You might have overdone it," Tim said.

"Orange Hill Cartel just wants them alive. They're alive."

"You are one lucky bastard," Tim said. "If your wife hadn't run you off, they would have stolen everything."

"You're right," Kennedy said. "And I still might get the chance to screw that little girl, so things are looking up." He glanced around the office. "Guard the door."

"They're locked in there with their hands tied."

"You're going to watch that door until the Orange Hill Cartel collects them. So make yourself comfortable."

"What are you going to do?"

"Take care of business."

Kennedy went back into his office, opened his safe, and put the banded bundles of money back inside. Then he sat down behind his desk. It was almost 5:00 a.m. back east. He got out his smartphone and speed-dialed Mr. Wishes.

"This better be good."

"Remember the grifter couple who stole your diamonds?"

"The ones who fenced them to you?"

"Yes. I've got them."

"You absolutely sure it's them?"

"Absolutely. Do you still want them?"

"You bet I do. I've been waiting for this pleasure a long time."

"What do you want me to do?"

"I'm coming to you. I'll text you when I know my timeline."

"I'll be waiting."

Kennedy walked back through his offices to the room he was using as his bedroom and lay down on the blowup mattress. Fucking grifters. But Tim was right. Brenda locking him out was the best luck he'd had in a long time. He'd saved his money and captured the grifters. Maybe the Orange Hill Cartel would be grateful. Maybe he'd be able to renegotiate his arrangement with them. He deserved more money. He deserved to be treated like a partner. Or maybe they should just let him go. That would be best of all. They didn't pay him nearly enough for the risk of handling their diamonds.

At 9:00 a.m. he heard a notification buzz on his phone. Text message from Mr. Wishes. He was on a private plane. He'd be landing at the Chicago Executive Airport at 11:30 a.m. Where was that? Kennedy googled it. In Wheeling, about twenty miles north of downtown. Kennedy rolled off the mattress and went into the bathroom to brush his teeth and splash water in his face. After he got dressed, he went down to the room where Tim was keeping guard. Tim was stretched out in a comfy chair with his feet up on a low table.

"Tim."

Tim opened his eyes and turned his head. "All good, boss."

"I'm going out. Keep your wits about you."

"Everything's under control."

"Want me to bring you anything?"

"A coffee and a muffin would be great."

Kennedy came out the front of the building, locking the door behind him, and walked around to the far side where he'd parked his Mercedes. He didn't know why he cared if his neighbors knew he was sleeping in his offices, but he did. He looked at his watch. He had enough time to stop for breakfast on his way to the airport.

· · ·

SMITH WATCHED Kennedy exit the building, disappear around the far side, and then reappear in his car. This situation was getting stranger and stranger. Kennedy hadn't come to the building since they'd been there, so he must have been in the building all night. The Suttons and Chrissie hadn't come out, so they were still in there. And the bearded guy, maybe an employee of Kennedy's, had gone in shortly after 3:00 a.m. He must still be in there as well. So at least four people were in the building. Was Kennedy in cahoots with the Suttons? Was it a fake robbery designed to look like the real thing? Had Chrissie lied to him about what was going on?

Smith sipped his cold coffee. Well, their objective was clear. Arrest the Suttons. They were in the building. The best option was still to wait until they came out, so they could take them in the open, avoid a gunfight, and not accidently harm Makarova or the bearded guy. There was no advantage to picking up Kennedy now. If they were expecting him to come back, and he didn't, that might make this situation even more complicated. The best thing to do was stick with their plan and sort out the players afterward.


WHEN RANDY WOKE, his head pounding, he was lying in the dark wondering where he was. Then the night before flooded back. "Jodi," he whispered. "Jodi, you awake?"

She moaned softly. "Yeah, I'm here."

"What about Chrissie?"

Chrissie started sobbing.

"Be quiet," Randy said. "We're not going to die here."

"I think I saw a light switch by the door," Jodi whispered.

"That's a start."

Randy squirmed over to the wall, shrugged up onto his feet, found the doorknob with his hip, and rubbed his shoulder along the wall until he found the switch. An overhead fluorescent tube lit up. "Good call, Jodi," he whispered.

He looked at the others. Jodi had a black eye. Chrissie had a bloody lump on her forehead. His jaw felt loose, but he still had all his teeth. He walked the few steps to them and whispered. "Can you stand?"

They both got to their feet. "Every part of my body hurts," Chrissie said.

"Come closer. We don't want them to hear us," Randy said. They all stood face to face. Randy continued. "The next thing we have to do is get our hands free."

They looked around the room. Vacuum cleaner, mop and bucket, broom, a row of wire shelves stacked with toilet paper, paper towels, a cleaning supply caddy, a case of coffee capsules, and printer paper. Nothing to cut the zip-ties.

"Jodi, turn around. I want to see what the zip ties look like."

She turned around.

"Okay, these aren't the heavy-duty police grade zip ties. They're just the hardware store version."

"So maybe we can break them?"

Randy pulled his hands up his back as high as he could, pushing his elbows away from his body, jumped in the air, and kicked his elbows out at hard as he could. His head spun. He leaned back against the wall. "Christ, that hurt."

Jodi nodded. "Always looks easier in the YouTube video."

He tried again. The zip-tie mechanism snapped and the zip tie fell to the floor. He rubbed his wrists.

"Me next?" Jodi asked.

"Let me see if I can find something to force the zip tie lock."

He dug through the cleaning caddie. Spray cleaner, window cleaner, roll of paper towels, a plastic scraper, and lying in the bottom, a flat-head screwdriver. "Come over to the shelf."

Jodi backed up to the wire shelves. Randy put her wrists up on the closest shelf, pushed the tip of the screwdriver into the locking mechanism of the zip tie, and twisted it. The zip tie slipped backward through the mechanism, loosening up enough for him to work the zip tie over her hands.

"Thanks," she whispered.

"Chrissie, your turn."

Chrissie backed up to the shelves. Randy used the screwdriver to loosen the zip tie and pulled it over her wrists.

"Okay," Randy said. "We need to be ready when they open the door."

"What can we do?" Chrissie looked around the room. "We've got a screwdriver and a broom handle. They've got guns."

Jodi rummaged through the boxes on the shelves and dumped out the cleaning caddie. "She's right. That's all we've got."

"Is there something we can wedge under the door? Maybe we can keep them out while we make a plan," Randy said.

"How about this?" Jodi held up a plastic scraper.

Randy shoved it under the door. "Too loose."

Chrissie looked at the cleaning products where Jodi had dumped them. "How about the trigger off this sprayer?"

She unscrewed it from the window cleaner bottle and handed it to Randy. He laid it down on the floor and tapped it into place with his boot. "That might slow them down."

"What's next?" Chrissie asked.

Randy looked at Jodi. "It's been a long time since we've been trapped in a room."

"Should have checked all the rooms before we went into the office," she replied.

"Would have, could have, should have. We've been out of rhythm ever since we set up Brighton. Too broke. Too willing to take chances."

"The police drone was just bad luck."

"Should have assumed that Brighton had resources." He glanced from Jodi to Chrissie. "Do either of you know how long we've been here?"

They shook their heads.

"We need to be gone before Mr. Wishes shows up."

"Who's Mr. Wishes?" Chrissie asked.

"Enforcer with the Orange Hill Cartel," Randy replied.

"We messed up their pipeline for transporting stolen diamonds," Jodi added.

"So he wants you dead," Chrissie said.

"Eventually." Randy looked around the room. "Drywall walls. Three sides on the inside of the building. Outside wall has sheet metal exterior."

"So we're not breaking through," Jodi said.

Chrissie pointed up. "What's above the hanging ceiling?"

Randy climbed up on the shelves and lifted a two-foot by two-foot panel out of the way. He waited a moment for his eyes to adjust to the dark. The roof support wall framing cut the building in half all the way up to the rafters. The rest of the interior walls tied into the support wall and the exterior walls just above the ceiling. Heating and cooling ductwork and electrical cabling snaked through the support wall framing and along the tops of the other walls. Wires hung from the rafters down to the drop ceiling grid. Randy climbed back into the room and explained what he'd seen.

"So we have to assume someone is watching the storeroom door," Jodi whispered.

"And the hanging ceiling won't support anyone's weight," Randy said.

"But we can tell where each of the rooms is."

Chrissie cut in. "So someone has got to walk on the top of the walls until they get to the nearest room where they can drop down and then sneak back to let us out."

Randy and Jodi nodded.

Chrissie looked at Randy. "So that leaves you out. You're more likely to lose your balance."

"Fair enough."

"I'm probably the most agile," she continued. "No offense, Jodi."

"No, you're probably right."

"But have you ever killed anyone?" Randy asked. "Shot them in cold blood from behind, because that might be on the menu. Either Kennedy or his guy."

"Why would I have to do that?"

"Because we're not leaving here without the money. They didn't call the cops. They're planning to kill us, so they're fair game." He turned to Jodi. "You're up."

She nodded. "The front half of the building is open, so that could be risky."

"Agreed."

"And I don't want to drop down into the room Kennedy's sleeping in, so the best bet is probably Kennedy's office."

Randy nodded. "It's risky, but everything's risky."

Jodi started climbing the shelves.

"Good luck," Chrissie whispered.

# 13

Jodi pulled herself up onto the side wall of the storeroom and let her eyes adjust. It was just as Randy had described it. She stood up on the wall, one foot in front of the other, and slipped through the nearest wires holding up the ceiling grid. Three more steps and she was at a corner. She squatted, taking advantage of the place where four walls came together, and focused as hard as she could on seeing through the gloom. There was another wall three feet away, so she was at the hall.

She breathed slowly, listening for any noise below her, but she heard nothing. She turned left and made her way to the next inter-section, placing each foot slowly and carefully, trying hard not to make a sound. This should be the outside wall to Kennedy's office. She squatted where the walls formed a T and listened. All she could hear was the hum of the fluorescent lights. She burrowed her fingers under the edge of the closest ceiling panel and eased it up a crack. The room below was dark, though light fell into it from the hall. She continued lifting the panel very slowly just in case someone was close by, but when she finally moved it out of the way, she was looking into Kennedy's empty office.

She dropped into the room like a cat, turned, and peeked out the door. No one was in the hall. The front room was dark. Light fell into the hall from the room outside of the storeroom. She stood listening. No one was talking, no one was moving. She turned to Kennedy's desk. What fucking hubris. He hadn't bothered to take away the things his guy had taken out of their pockets, and their duffel still sat on the floor. This was why he was meant to be robbed.

She picked up Randy's revolver. The weight told her it was still loaded. Then she picked up her smartphone. It was 11:00 a.m. They were running out of time. She moved slowly down the hall, the gun in front of her with her left hand supporting her right wrist. She peeked into the room outside of the storeroom. Kennedy's guy sat in an easy chair, his eyes closed, the AR-15 lying on the table within easy reach. Jodi snuck up behind him and cocked the hammer on the revolver as she pressed the barrel against his ear. His eyes snapped open.

"Don't move," she said.

He tried to see her out of the corner of his eye.

"You're still alive. It's up to you if you stay that way. Slowly put your hands under your thighs."

He did as he was told.

"Good choice. Where's the key to the storeroom?"

"On the table."

She stepped around him, the revolver pointed at his chest, picked up the AR-15 rifle, put the revolver in her belt, and then picked up the key.

"I want to cooperate," he said.

"Then keep sitting there. Where's Kennedy?"

"He left."

"Is that the truth?"

"Like I said, I want to cooperate."

She backed up to the storeroom door and banged on it. "I'm here." She put the key in the doorknob lock, unlocked the door, and moved into the room. The door swung open behind her. Randy and Chrissie rushed out of the storeroom.

"Kennedy?" Randy asked.

"Not here." Jodi handed him the revolver.

"I'm checking the other rooms," Randy said.

"It's after eleven."

"Jesus."

Randy disappeared into the hall. Jodi looked at Kennedy's guy. He was wearing lace-up gym shoes. "Slip off those shoes."

"They're on tight. I need to untie them first."

She shook her head. "You stop sitting on your hands, you're going to get shot."

He managed to pry his shoes off using his feet. Jodi turned to Chrissie. "Get the laces out of his shoes."

Christie removed the laces.

Jodi spoke to Kennedy's guy. "Now then. You're going to get up very slowly and walk into the storeroom where you're going to lay down on your stomach."

"What are you going to do?"

"Save your life."

Jodi kept the rifle pointed at him while she followed him into the storeroom where he lay down. Chrissie tied his ankles together and his hands behind his back. Randy came back into the room. "No one is here."

"Then it's time to take the money," Jodi said.

"This guy tied down tight?"

"He's not getting loose," Chrissie said.

"Let's get moving," Jodi said.

They locked the bodyguard in the storeroom. "Chrissie," Randy said, "you watch from the front door."

"Right after I get my stuff back."

They all went back to Kennedy's office. Randy turned the lights on. They all pocketed the rest of their personal items. "Scoot," Randy said to Chrissie. She took off down the hall.

Randy glanced around the room. "Where's the index finger?"

They searched the bookshelves and looked in the trashcan. Jodi found it under the desk.

"We're in business now," Randy said. He turned to the safe.

. . .

Meanwhile, Kennedy sat on a sofa in the lounge at the Chicago Executive Airport, waiting for Mr. Wishes' plane to taxi to the gate. A woman and a man, dressed in airline employee uniforms, stood behind the counter near the doors. Would Mr. Wishes be in a good mood? Good enough that he'd be willing to cut a deal? Would he expect his help getting rid of the grifters?

Mr. Wishes, black clothes and a small carry-on bag, nodded at Kennedy as he strode into the lounge, heading for the glass doors to the parking lot. Kennedy got up and fell in beside him. "How was your flight?"

Mr. Wishes glanced at him as if he was an idiot. "It was a flight. Where have you got them?"

"Under guard and locked in a storeroom."

"Out at your offices?"

"Yeah."

"Can you get me some copper wire, heavy duty rubber gloves, and a plastic apron?"

"On the way or after I drop you?"

"On the way. I want to be in and out of here as quickly as possible."

Randy and Jodi stood in front of the safe in Kennedy's office, Jodi holding the ripstop bag and Randy stuffing it with banded bundles of bills.

Jodi chuckled. "Leave the index finger inside?"

Randy nodded.

"What about the gems and the bearer bonds?"

"Didn't want the trouble originally, but now I'd rather get ten cents on the dollar than let Kennedy keep them."

He zipped up the bag and tossed it behind them. Jodi got another bag out of their tool duffel. Randy slid the folder of bearer bonds onto the bottom and then dumped three trays of gems on top. "That's all of it."

Jodi tossed the prosthetic finger into the empty safe, and Randy shut the door. "Do you think the cops are waiting for us?" Jodi asked.

"We have to assume they are."

"Even though the bodyguard came in and Kennedy went out?"

"The cops could be holding Kennedy right now. Chrissie's got that burner phone. Either she's been talking to Smith or Brighton or she's got other partners. More than likely she's working with the cops. Right now would be the best opportunity to ambush us and take the loot."

"You're right. What should we do with her?"

"She doesn't know where we're going from here. Better for us if she's alive with Kennedy and the cartel chasing her."

Randy picked up the tool duffel and Jodi shouldered both ripstop bags. They started down the hall toward the front office, watching Chrissie as she stood at the door.

"Have you got the money?" Chrissie asked.

"Got it all," Randy said.

"Is anyone out there?" Jodi asked.

"Just the bodyguard's jeep," Chrissie said.

Randy cracked the door open and scanned the area. It was a beautiful sunny fall day. The Dodge Dakota still sat in the parking space where they had left it. To the right, two FedEx delivery vans were backed up to the loading dock of the FedEx warehouse. The parking lot contained three cars; plus the tan Camry they'd parked there yesterday. To the left, the call center lot was full, and a taco truck was parked near the picnic tables at the near side of the building, where four people were having an early lunch. All civilians going about their business. But something didn't feel right. Randy looked again, studying the call center lot. At the far end of the lot, in a parking spot that was a straight shot onto Prairie View Avenue, he saw a black Ford Explorer. Lots of people owned them, but it was a classic FBI vehicle. He looked down the street in the other direction at an anonymous office building. Five parked cars and a dumpster. He squinted. Was that the front edge of a vehicle bumper peeking out from behind the dumpster? Was he just being paranoid? This was no time to take a chance. Being paranoid now only made you look foolish later, while not being paranoid might put you in jail. He looked back at the FedEx parking lot. It looked like the best bet.

"We're not going out the front," he said.

"Why not? The truck is right there," Chrissie said.

"I don't like it."

"So we're moving to the backup plan," Jodi said.

Randy spotted the bodyguard's workstation, where an all-in-one desktop computer sat on an Ikea desk. "We cut the fiber optic cable on our way in, so the only surveillance footage of us that's not a couple of minutes of dark blur would have to be on the hard drive of this computer."

"Why care?" Chrissie asked. "Kennedy knows you were here."

"Because we don't want to leave any evidence for the cops," Randy replied.

"You think the cops are out there?"

"Wouldn't be surprised." Randy turned to Jodi. "Smash it."

She swung the computer over her head and threw it down. Then she jumped up and down on it until the components made tinkling sounds when she stomped. "That's the best I can do unless you want me to shoot through the hard drive."

"No shots," Randy said. "We need to keep the element of surprise."

"There's nobody out there," Chrissie said.

"Back door," Randy said to Jodi.

They went through the offices to the emergency exit at the back of the building.

"Okay, we slip around the right side of the building, moving fast, stay in the cover of the building as long as possible, and then run for the Camry."

Jodi pulled the revolver from her belt and pointed it at Chrissie. "You're not coming."

"What? You can't be serious."

"We know about the burner phone," Jodi replied.

"What are you talking about?"

"The burner phone," Randy said. "The one you've been using to rat us out."

"I didn't rat on you. You can't do this. I need my cut."

"What cut? Rats don't get a cut."

Chrissie started crying.

"You really know how to sell it, kid. But I'm not buying it." Randy pointed to the front of the building. "You think it's safe out front? Get in the Dakota and run."

"What are you talking about?"

"Kennedy knows who you are. And the Orange Hill Cartel will want revenge."

"And you're going to stiff me?"

"You made your choice," Randy said. "I was in jail. Jodi was having to do favors for that dope-slinging pimp. She was lucky to break me out. You chose the wrong side."

"You can't leave me here."

"You follow us, you're going to get shot."

Randy pushed open the back door, the duffel over his shoulder and the rifle in a two-handed position. Jodi came after him with a ripstop bag in each hand.

IN THE CUL-DE-SAC, the FBI agent in the passenger's seat of the Explorer tapped his comms. "Suttons are on the move. Running for the FedEx parking lot."

"Go, go, go," Smith replied.

The three Ford Explorers, red and blue lights pulsing, raced across Prairie View Avenue into Kennedy's parking lot.

RANDY AND JODI ran flat out across the grass to the FedEx parking lot. When they got to the Camry, Randy pulled a small tablet from the gear duffel to mimic the car key fob and start the Camry's engine.

They tossed their bags inside and jumped in. Randy jammed the car into Drive and stomped on the gas pedal, gaining speed as he approached Prairie View Avenue. Two of the Explorers flipped on their sirens and started after them. They jumped the curb, shot across the grass, and bounced down into the FedEx parking lot. Randy squealed out of the parking lot, turning right. Jodi looked over her shoulder. "There's two of them behind us."

Randy sped through the red light on the boulevard, weaving through the traffic in the intersection. A minivan braked hard, slid sideways, and tapped the Camry's bumper before it slammed into the side of the first Explorer.

Jodi looked over her shoulder. "One of the Explorers is down. The other one is still coming."

Randy turned left into a neighborhood, right at the end of the block, and then right again. Jodi couldn't see the Explorer, but they could hear its siren in the distance.

"Maybe we've lost them."

"We need to ditch this car. Find another."

Jodi scanned the sides of the street. "There's a red Sentry up ahead."

"I see it." Randy slid in behind the Sentra and turned off the Camry. They rushed out of the car with the duffel and the rip-stop bags and ran up to the doors on the Sentra. After Randy used the tablet to open the car and start the engine, Jodi tossed their bags into the back seat.

Randy drove up to the first corner and turned right. "That was close."

"Too close. Chrissie deserves whatever happens to her."


BACK AT KENNEDY'S OFFICES, Chrissie sat on the parking lot curb near the sidewalk to the building entrance with her hands cuffed behind her back. Two FBI agents were leading the bodyguard out of the building. Agent Smith stood nearby, talking on his phone with the agents who were still looking for Randy and Jodi. After he put his phone away, he led Chrissie to the trunk of the Ford Taurus. "Let's hear your story one more time."

"It's not a story."

"You came here with the Suttons to rob the safe."

"I came here because you told me to come here."

"Kennedy surprised you, called his bodyguard, and locked you in a closet."

"Beat us with a broom handle."

"You escaped and locked up the bodyguard. Kennedy was gone."

"Exactly. Randy was suspicious. Accused me of being a rat. Left me and went out the back of the building. You guys charged in."

"Turn around."

She turned toward the trunk and he uncuffed her.

"Ms. Makarova, you held up your end of the bargain. You're free to go."

"Free to go? You really screwed me."

"You screwed yourself. God knows what you were really up to here, but a deal's a deal."

"Can I have my stuff back?"

He opened the trunk and got out a plastic bag that contained her phone, her wallet, and a package of tissues and handed it to her. "If we have any more questions, we'll be in touch." Smith walked over to the two agents standing with the bodyguard.

Chrissie watched him walk away. Why did she always end up so screwed? Still no money. The Suttons on the loose. At least the election would be over in three weeks, Terry would settle down, and she'd be able to get her escort job back. She needed to get back to her car at the motel. She put her wallet and tissues in her pockets and called a rideshare. Was Randy telling the truth? Would Kennedy and the Orange Hill Cartel think she'd stolen their cash? Did she really need to run? They didn't know where she was from, didn't know her name—there was no way they could find her once she disappeared. All she had to do was make sure no one saw her with her car. As she walked over to the entrance to the parking lot to wait for her rideshare, a CSI van rolled into the lot.

. . .

KENNEDY AND MR. WISHES were on the boulevard near Kennedy's offices when they spotted the tow trucks clearing the wrecked cars from the intersection to Prairie View Avenue. "I don't like the look of this," Mr. Wishes said.

Kennedy turned onto Prairie View Avenue. As they approached his offices, they saw the FBI Ford Explorer and the CSI van in the parking lot. "Keep going," Mr. Wishes said.

Kennedy turned around in the cul-de-sac and drove back out onto the boulevard. At the next intersection, he pulled into a Perkins restaurant. "Wait here while I go find out what's going on."

Mr. Wishes got out of the car. Kennedy drove back down to his offices and pulled into the parking lot. Tim, accompanied by an FBI agent in tactical gear, walked toward him when he got out of his Mercedes.

"What's going on?" he asked.

"Mr. Kennedy?" the agent asked.

"Yes."

He showed his ID. Special Agent Joseph Smith. "You've got a very interesting situation here."

"What do you mean?"

"An escaped criminal wanted for murder was in your offices along with two accomplices."

He turned to Tim. "What's he talking about?"

"Some people were hiding in the building. They jumped me after you left."

"My God. Are you okay?"

"Yeah. They locked me in the storeroom."

"Did you see their faces?"

"They were wearing masks."

Kennedy turned to Agent Smith. "And you were here?"

"We had a tip they were in the building."

"And they got away?"

"So you didn't know that they had broken in to your offices?"

"No idea."

"What would you say if I told you that a confidential informant reported that you captured the Suttons and they escaped after you left?"

Kennedy glanced at Tim. He shook his head no. "I'd say your informant was a liar."

"Where did you go when you left here?"

"Just drove around to get some fresh air."

"Why did this man come here at four a.m.?"

"I think I've answered enough questions," Kennedy said. He turned to Tim. "Have we been robbed?"

"I don't know," Tim said. "The FBI brought me out of the storeroom."

"I need to look in my safe."

"We're not done talking."

"I'm not saying anything else without my lawyer. I have a right to go into my offices. Can I please look in my safe?"

"Let me check with CSI." Smith took out his phone and made a call. When he was done, he handed Kennedy a pair of throwaway gloves. "I'll take you in. CSI is still working. Don't touch anything without their okay."

Smith led Kennedy into the building. All the lights were on. CSI techs dressed in white coveralls were dusting for fingerprints and using scanners to hunt for blood splatter. In the front office, Tim's computer was smashed. Kennedy tried to act as if he was surprised as he made his way back to his office. The safe was locked, but that didn't mean anything. He turned to the nearest CSI tech. "Can I open my safe?"

He nodded. "We've already dusted."

Kennedy dialed in the combination, took off one glove to scan his index finger, and then unbolted the door. Smith watched from over his shoulder.

The safe was empty except for a plastic model of a finger. No cash, no gems, no Orange Hill Cartel diamonds, no bearer bonds. He picked up the finger and examined it. "Christ. They cleaned me out. Everything's gone. My inventory. My onsite cash. Everything."

"I'm sorry to hear it," Smith said. "Do you have records that will prove what was in there?"

"My books show what I purchased and what I sold. My bank account shows my deposits. The difference is what was in the safe."

"You'll need to provide those records."

"I can have them by tomorrow." He rubbed his face. "My God, what am I going to do?"

He walked out of the building and sat down in his car. He should have killed the grifters when he had the chance. Then he'd still have his gems and money and the cartel's diamonds. But even then he'd be screwed, because the FBI had been watching the building. They would have caught him with the bodies. The cops or the cartel? Which was worse? He called Mr. Wishes.

"Yes," he said.

"The grifters took everything."

"Everything?"

"They cleaned out my safe. There's nothing left. No diamonds, no cash, nothing."

"I'm putting my guys on the grifters. In the meantime, you're going to have to make a plan to pay us back."

"But you told me to keep the diamonds in the safe."

"Not my problem. I'm going back to the airport. Get in touch when you've got our money." Mr. Wishes ended the call.

Kennedy tossed his phone into the passenger's seat. That rat bastard. What was he going to do? He still had his legitimate resources—the money he kept in the bank and the gems he stored in the safe deposit box—so he could still do business, even if he'd lost the bearer bonds and his illegal gems. But he was deep in the hole if he had to make up for the cartel's diamonds. To get that kind of cash, he'd have to get into the Cayman bank account, and that meant crawling back to Brenda to get her cooperation. What a shit storm.

Tim tapped on his window. He lowered it.

"What do you want me to do, boss?"

"Stay here until the cops are done, then give me a call before you lock up."

SMITH STOOD in the parking lot and watched Kennedy drive away. Kennedy and his guy were both lying. Makarova had the bruises to prove she'd been beaten, and her story fit the timeline. She'd arrived with the Suttons just before 2:00 a.m. Kennedy's guy had arrived around 4:00 a.m. Kennedy had left after 9:00 a.m. The Suttons and Makarova came out of the building at 11:45 a.m. Kennedy must have called his guy. He left him guarding the Suttons and Makarova. Where did he go? Was he meeting someone or preparing a kill zone? Or were he, the Suttons, and Makarova all in it together? Did the Suttons go out the back of the building knowing the FBI was watching? Was the plan to split the contents of the safe and the insurance money? He needed to interrogate Kennedy and his guy until he found an inconsistency he could use to force the truth out of Makarova.

KENNEDY DROVE HOME, pulled up into the garage, and went into the house through the kitchen. Upstairs he found Brenda in their bedroom, still in her workout clothes.

"What are you doing here? I'm still angry with you."

He stood in the center of the room with his hands in his pockets. "The offices have been robbed."

"You're making that up."

"They cracked the safe."

"You expect me to believe that? As many times as you've told me that safe was uncrackable?"

"The FBI are there right now. CSI. The works."

"Really?"

"Really."

She sat on the edge of the bed. "Do you think the FBI will catch them?"

"I hope so, but I'm not holding my breath."

"But we still have money?"

"The money at the bank and in the Cayman account."

"So life goes on."

"I need to repay some clients."

"With our money?"

"I'll make it back later."

She studied him for a moment. Then she smiled. "So that's why you're here. You need me to access the Cayman account."

He shrugged.

"If you want my help, you're going to give up Rhonda and the love nest."

"I'm not sleeping with Rhonda. I just like the way she cuts my hair. You haven't got anything to be jealous about."

"Then why does Rhonda's husband think something is going on?"

"I don't know."

"You can stand here and lie to my face all you want, but I won't help you until you show me a terminated lease and can account for every minute of your day."

"And I can come back into the bedroom?"

"Maybe. After you take an STD test."

"An STD test?"

"That's what it will take. I don't know who you've been with besides Rhonda, and I'm not taking any chances. Until then, you're sleeping down the hall."

"But I haven't been with anyone."

"You're such a bad liar, Jackson. You're going to admit what you've done and you're going to do what I ask, or you're not going to get access to the Cayman account."

"You're such a bitch."

"And you're a narcissistic asshole. The sooner you do what I ask, the sooner you'll have the money you need."

"You just want me to kiss your ass."

"You got that exactly right. And you're going to kiss my ass until I'm satisfied you've groveled enough."

Kennedy stomped down the stairs and back into the garage. Brenda had him by the balls and she knew it. He had to pay back the Orange Hill Cartel as soon as possible, or they'd make his life a lot more miserable than Brenda could. He was going to have to break the lease at the apartment, make a show of not seeing Rhonda, get the STD test. Play nice until Brenda let her guard down. Make her believe he could change. But this was the last straw. He needed to start hiding assets in preparation for a divorce. He'd lose the house, her car, half the cash in the bank for sure. But there were plenty of assets he could hide, depending on how he structured his business deals. He needed an office and a safe she didn't know about. One that a private investigator wouldn't be able to find.

LATER THAT DAY, Smith sat in the chair facing Agent Cooper's desk. Cooper had a deep frown on his face.

"What did I tell you was going to happen if you screwed this job up?"

"That you were going to paint me with it."

"And here we are. A local businessman robbed and the murderers still on the loose."

"Kennedy was up to no good. His actions have conspiracy written all over them."

"Do you have any proof? Anything concrete?"

"If you let me bring him in, I'll get the proof."

"You're suspended pending an investigation of your actions in this matter. Not just in Chicago, but from the very beginning in Ohio."

"Everything I did was completely aboveboard."

"You could do yourself a favor and take early retirement."

"I don't have enough points."

"Then you really are screwed. I'm putting a team on the Suttons. If you get anywhere near this investigation, you'll be wishing you were still building time in some backwater."

"Yes, sir."

"Get out of here."

Smith took the elevator down to the lobby. This case had looked so promising right up until it turned to mud. He would have been in better shape if he'd green-lit an assault on a motel, three people had died, and he'd captured the Suttons. He pushed through the revolving door. The sidewalk was busy with pedestrians and the street was stop-and-go traffic. He stepped back to the side of the building. Better warn Brighton. He took out his phone.

"Terry?"

"Smitty. Good news I hope."

"The Suttons got away. I'm on suspension, and I'm being investigated. They'll be going over everything we did."

"They're going to look at the blackmail?"

"Everything I was involved with."

"Christ. I'm glad I destroyed that tablet."

"It could still be tricky."

"Don't lie, but don't give anything away. That's the trick. If you lie, you're going to get caught."

"I know the drill."

"You coming home?"

"I'll be on the next flight."

"We'll get through this."

"I hope so."

"I look after my friends, Smitty."

"I appreciate it, Terry."

"Keep your head down until after the election. Then I'll do everything I can to keep you in the clear. Get in touch when you're back in town, and we'll get our ducks in a row."

Smith walked down to the corner and ordered a rideshare. Fucking Suttons. They had a four hour head start. They had plenty of money. If they got a clean car and a new set of IDs, they'd be almost impossible to find. Well, not his problem anymore. Someone else could take the credit or the blame.

· · ·

RANDY AND JODI pulled off Interstate 94 at a Casey's General Store near Madison, Wisconsin, to buy snacks and gas. The place was busy, but no one in the parking lot or the convenience store looked like someone they should worry about—just the usual assortment of travelers going about their business.

After they filled the Sentra's tank, used the restrooms, and bought chips and iced tea, they got back on the road, headed for Minnesota. "That was a good call back at Kennedy's, baby," Jodi said.

"It was time we caught a break."

"And we made a pile. Wonder what the gems are worth?" she asked.

"The discount is going to be a killer. Even then it will be hard to find someone to take them after the Orange Hill Cartel puts the word out."

She laughed. "But we've got the bearer bonds and the cash to tide us over, so waiting for the right opportunity shouldn't be a problem."

"You seem very happy."

"I am. I like being rich. How long are we going to keep this car?"

"Runs good. Let's keep it until Minneapolis, then we'll find a nice quiet parking lot where we can trade out," Randy said.

"How far do you want to run?"

"Until I'm sure the Orange Hill Cartel and the Feds can't find us."

Jodi opened her bottle of iced tea. "We need fresh documents."

"I know. But we've got plenty of cash now, so it's not a problem. How about we try Smithdale? He does quality work."

"Is he still alive?"

"Don't know. He was still spry the last time."

Jodi pulled up a map app on her phone. "Okay, so at Minneapolis we cut down I-35 to get to I-80."

"Sounds like a plan. We'll stop for dinner along the way. We need to keep moving until we have new documents."

## 14

Three days later, Mr. Wishes was sitting in a poorly lit booth in the back of the Atlas Tavern, sipping on a rum and Coke and talking with a Black man and a Black woman who were dressed like accountants.

"The cops found the Camry on a side street," the man said. "An old Sentra was reported stolen off that block the same day as the robbery. We found the Sentra at the Mall of America in Bloomington, Minnesota. Nothing on the security cameras."

"The grifters didn't just fall off the earth, Sean."

"No, sir. And we're still looking. Now the girl, on the other hand, she's got no skills at all."

"Where is she?"

"She called her mom at a care center yesterday. We traced the call back to Putney, Ohio."

"Pay her a visit."

RANDY AND JODI sat in a stolen Toyota Camry in the on-street parking in front of Smithdale Photography in Deer Park, Colorado, at 6:00

p.m. The shop was open, even though most of the other stores downtown were already closed.

"How does it look to you?" Randy asked.

Jodi glanced up and down the street. Two teenagers went into the pharmacy on the corner, and a minivan backed out of a parking space in front of an Every-Sport shoe store. "No red flags."

"Let's get this done."

A bell sounded when they opened the door to the photography shop. Inside, family portraits and High School Senior photos lined the walls. An elderly man with stooped shoulders and thick glasses, red suspenders holding up his pants, came out of the backroom and stood behind the counter. "As I live and breathe," he said.

Jodi smiled. "Robert. You haven't aged a day since last time."

"Then I'm not the only one who needs glasses." He wiped at the counter with a rag. "What can I do for you?"

"Need a full package," Randy said. "Need it as soon as possible."

"Driver's licenses and passports I can have by tomorrow. Credit cards with chips will take longer."

"Skip the cards. Will the passports stand up to a passport control scanner?"

"Only the best work for you two. You got pictures?"

"No."

"Come on back into the studio."

AFTER DINNER, Randy and Jodi were sitting at the round table by the window in their motel room, looking at the screen on Jodi's laptop. They'd just finished watching a short clip from the video of Chrissie and Brighton in the motel room.

"That's Brighton with his junk out, no doubt about it," Randy said. "And that's definitely Chrissie's body in profile, showing off her lady parts and the little-girl costume."

"But her face is turned, so no one knows who she is."

"And that's the way you want to do it?"

Jodi nodded. "Brighton's got it coming. He decided to play hard-ball, so he gets hardball."

"We promised to release the video if he didn't pay."

"Exactly."

"Chrissy double-crossed us."

"She did."

"Twice."

"I know. But she's not really a player. And being a woman with your private bits on the internet when it's not something you chose— I just can't show her face."

"So you want to give her a pass?"

"That's where I land."

"Okay, I'll go along."

"We need to put this video clip someplace where it won't be taken down."

"How about Pornhub? Then we send the link to the reporter at the *Putney Tribune*."

"And all the county and city officials."

Randy chuckled. "You've got a mean streak when it comes to Brighton."

She smiled. "Learned it from you."

"Brighton is definitely losing the election."

Jodi logged into PornHub using a phony email account and uploaded the video clip. Then she emailed the reporter and the local officials with the link. "All done." She closed her laptop.

"You've really upped your computer game."

"I'm no expert, but I try to keep up."

"Well, now we're done with paybacks," Randy said. "Wonder how long it will take for Brighton's campaign to blow up?"

"Couple of days, I imagine."

"Now we just need to focus on our future."

"We're lucky Robert is still working," Jodi said.

"We're lucky Robert is still alive," Randy replied. "Not many real artists left."

"Are we going to spend the night here tomorrow after we get the new papers, or are we going to head straight out of town?"

"The tourist season is over. Let's go up to Estes Park. Get an Airbnb on the new IDs. Lay low for a week."

THE NEXT DAY, Chrissie, wearing a hoodie and yoga pants and carrying a gym bag, was walking home from the Putney State University recreation center after her core workout. She had a short timeline to shower and get dressed for her bartending shift. Ms. Gleason at the escort service was still not talking to her, but she was confident she'd have her old job back as soon as the election was over.

As she turned the corner and started down the street to her house, she was glad Agent Smith's Ford Explorer wasn't parked at the curb. The last thing she needed was him trying to involve her in another fiasco. A Black man and a Black woman, dress clothes and overcoats, bibles in their hands, were standing on the neighbor's stoop. As Chrissie started up her own sidewalk, the woman called to her.

"Ma'am," she said, "ma'am, have you got a minute?" The woman hurried across the grass toward her. "I've got some news that will change your life."

Chrissie put her key in her front door lock. "I'm not interested."

The woman was standing behind her. "Are you sure? I'll only take a minute of your time."

"I'm late for work."

Chrissie pushed her door open. The woman came in behind her. "Hey!"

The woman dropped the bible and pressed a snub-nosed revolver into Chrissie's stomach. The man came in and shut the door.

"What's going on? There's nothing to steal here."

The man snapped his fingers in front of her face. "Pay attention. Anyone else home? We don't want to accidently kill one of your roommates."

Chrissie looked from the man to the woman to the revolver. "There's no one here."

"Sit down," the woman said. She kept the gun against Chrissie's stomach as she backed her onto the sofa.

The man dumped out her gym bag. Gym shoes, student ID, yoga strap. "Nothing here."

"Give me your phone," the woman said.

Chrissie handed her the phone.

"Open it."

Chrissie used face ID.

The woman stepped back and went through Chrissie's phone, checking the texts and the past calls. "Nothing here."

The man dragged a chair over and sat facing Chrissie, their knees almost touching. "You know why we're here?"

She shook her head.

"You were with the grifters in Chicago."

"Randy and Jodi?"

"Whatever they were calling themselves. You all stole our goods."

"Not me. That was them. They took everything and left me there."

"Is that right?"

"You think I'd have a shitty bartending job if I had a cut of the cash or the gems out of that safe?"

The man nodded thoughtfully. The woman bent down and smacked Chrissie across the face. Her head snapped back and tears sprang from her eyes.

"You must know something," the woman said.

"I don't know anything."

"I don't want to break your fingers or cut your face."

"I'd tell you if I knew."

"A cut-faced girl can't do escort work."

"I don't know anything."

The man stood up, took out his phone, and went into the hall. "Mr. Wishes?"

"Speak."

"This girl is as weak as water. She doesn't know anything."

"I'm not surprised. It's the way these grifters operate."

"Clean her up?"

"We don't need the headache of dealing with the body. She's not going to talk or be in the way."

The man went back into the living room. "Your lucky day," he said to Chrissie. He turned to the woman. "Let's go."

"Really?"

"Uh-huh."

He turned back to Chrissie. "Stay out of the game."

The woman picked up the bible from the floor and they left, leaving the door wide open.

Chrissie sat for a moment looking through the open door, the cool night air rushing into the house. *Jesus. Jesus. Jesus.* She'd almost been tortured and murdered. She got up and shut the door before she shoved her things back into her gym bag and went down the hall to the bathroom. She looked in the mirror. Her cheek was still red, but it didn't look like it was going to bruise. Those gangsters must have been connected to Kennedy. Should she call Agent Smith? She turned on the cold water tap and splashed water on her face. No, that would just make things worse. She needed to keep her head down. She went back into the living room and picked up her phone. No time for a shower. She'd have to wipe her armpits and put on more deodorant. She had to get moving. She couldn't afford to lose this job.

MEANWHILE, Randy input the passcode on the door lock of the condo in Estes Park, Colorado, that Jodi had booked that morning after they picked up their new IDs. The condo sat on a hillside. The front door was on the street at the upper part of the hill. The living room was wood paneling with a mountain stone fireplace and a view of the near mountains. A patio door led to a deck that contained a round metal table and two chairs and overlooked a parking lot on the lower side of the hill. They left their roller bags by the door, glanced in the galley kitchen, and then walked through to the bedroom suite, where a flatscreen TV hung on the wall opposite the king-size bed.

"Very livable," Randy said.

Jodi glanced into the huge bathroom. "We could hold a party in here."

"Maybe we will."

They walked back through to the living room and out onto the deck. The parking lot below was half-empty. "Lots of peace and quiet."

He sat down in one of the chairs. "Okay. What do we need?"

Jodi sat down in the other chair. "Groceries, another car, burner phones, Bluetooth door alarm. How much cash do we have?"

"One hundred and thirty-seven thousand dollars."

"We need a bank account and debit and credit cards."

"Tomorrow morning we'll go down the mountain to Loveland, set up an account at a bank there. Deposit five thousand."

"We'll need to find a used car place that will take cash."

Randy nodded. "And we need to divide up our stash, separate the cash from the gems and the bonds."

"Nobody's going to find us."

"Famous last words."

"Okay," Jodi said. "Let's keep the cash and our gear with us. Cut a slit in the box springs cover and put the gems and bonds inside."

"That means if we have to run, we'll have to circle back to the condo."

"What else can we do?"

"You're right," Randy said. "It's as good a plan as any for now."

"Only downside is that if we get stopped by the police with the cash and the weapons in our car, we'll be in trouble."

"We'll just have to take that chance. If we get ambushed, we'll need the guns and tactical gear."

TWO DAYS LATER, Sean and Phyllis, the Black couple who'd visited Chrissie, walked through the door of Smithdale Photography. A white-haired man wearing a bow tie stood behind the counter. "Can I help you?"

"Are you Robert Smithdale?" Sean asked.

"Who's asking?"

"We're fans of your work."

"I don't hear that very often." He pointed to framed photographs hanging on the walls. "I do pretty traditional poses."

"That's not the work we're talking about."

Sean stepped up to the counter and showed Smithdale a photo of Randy and Jodi taken from the video surveillance camera outside the Loveland Security Bank in Loveland, Colorado. "You know these two?"

"Don't believe I do."

"They were in here in the last few days."

"If you say so."

"You made them new IDs."

"I don't know what you're talking about."

Phyllis locked the front door to the shop and put up the *Closed* sign.

Sean continued. "Mr. Smithdale, we traced them to this area. You're the only real forger around here. So they had to come to you. We need to know their new names, and we need to know where they are."

"You're going to tell us," Phyllis said. "So you might as well do it without getting hurt first."

Sean shrugged. "We're going to find them anyway. It'll just be quicker."

"Or we could pick up your granddaughter from school and then come back," Phyllis added.

"You wouldn't really do that," Smithdale said.

"Your granddaughter, your grandson, your daughter—makes no difference to us," Sean replied.

"I don't know how the information could help you. They're long gone by now anyway."

"Then there's no reason you shouldn't tell us." Sean stepped around the counter, grabbed Smithdale by the front of his shirt, and pushed him into the wall. "Time's up."

"Make it easy on yourself," Phyllis added. "They're not worth it."

"Okay, okay, I'll tell you their names. I don't know where they went."

"It's the smart move," Sean said. "Write the names down for me."

Smithdale got a piece of note paper from a drawer and wrote down the names.

"I find out these aren't the right names, I'm going to be mad."

"Those are the names."

"I hope so."

Phyllis unlocked the front door and put up the *Open* sign before they headed down the sidewalk to where they'd parked their car. "Now we know what their new names are," Phyllis said.

"And we know they did some banking in Loveland."

"Maybe setting up an account."

"Do you think our guy could hack the bank?"

"He hacked the city's surveillance system. The bank couldn't be much tougher."

"Give him a call."

THE NEXT MORNING at 9:00 a.m., FBI Agent James Powers knocked on the door of the Loveland Security Bank. A young woman looked at him through the glass door.

"We open at ten. You can use the drive-through or the cash machine."

Powers held his ID up to the glass. The woman squinted as she read it, then she unlocked the door and held it open.

"I'm here to see the manager."

"Yes, sir. Follow me."

She led him through the lobby to an office to the left of the tellers' counter. "Ms. Larabee, the FBI agent is here."

A middle-aged woman wearing a blue pantsuit and a lot of jewelry stood up from behind her desk. "Thanks for coming. Have a seat." She pointed to the chair facing her desk. "Coffee?"

Powers sat down. "No thanks. I understand you had a security breach."

"Well, that's the thing. We're not sure. It's very peculiar."

"Go on."

"As you might imagine, we have an extensive firewall guarding our data. The automatic systems alerted us that someone had broken in, but when our I.T. specialists examined our computer programs and data, nothing important had been stolen or altered."

"How do you know it's not just a glitch?"

"They say *no*."

"So where's the crime?"

"Whoever broke in stole the names and addresses of people who opened an account this week."

"That's all?"

"That's all."

"No social security numbers, account numbers, or passwords?"

"No. Those are in encrypted files that weren't accessed."

"Can you give me the list of names and addresses?"

"Sure. Let me print it off." She opened a screen on her computer and clicked on the print icon.

"So, basically," Powers said, "you're just giving us the heads up in case this turns into something."

"Yes. Didn't want to wait for everything to go bad."

"Keep us in the loop."


BRIGHTON WAS SITTING in his office studying some court papers when his personal smartphone beeped. He looked at the screen. It was the investigative reporter from the *Putney Tribune*. She probably wanted a quote about the election. The race was closer than he liked, but he was still well in the lead. He took the call.

"Mr. Brighton?"

"How can I help you?"

"Are you aware that there's a video of you on PornHub?"

"That's crazy."

"If it's not you, it could be your doppelganger."

"Impossible."

"Engaged in sex acts with what appears to be an underage girl."

"It's not me."

"Is that your comment? I'll text you the link. You look at it and call me back." She ended the call.

Brighton saw the text from the reporter and clicked on the link. Sure enough, the link led to PornHub. He clicked on the video. It was him, naked, full-frontal. Chrissie in the schoolgirl outfit, her face always turned away. No way to claim it was her, prove she was of age. No way to claim they weren't having sex, that the video was out of context.

He looked around the website. There didn't appear to be any way for him to easily delete it. *Christ.* Who did he know who could figure this out and keep their mouth shut?

His phone rang again. It was the reporter.

"Any comment?"

"It's not me."

"The election is in two weeks. How do you think this will affect the results?"

"Voters are sophisticated enough to realize videos like this are easy to fake. That's not me. I'm confident I'll be reelected."

"Thank you." She ended the call.

Brighton set his phone down on his desk. Who could he call? Smitty was his go-to guy for these sorts of things, and he was still being investigated for the Sutton fiasco. His landline phone rang.

"Yes?"

"The mayor is on the line. Should I put him through?"


THAT AFTERNOON, Sean and Phyllis walked down the second-floor hall of a Holiday Inn Express, where Sean knocked on the door of room 216. Mr. Wishes opened the door. "You must have news."

They stepped into the room.

"Well?"

"Got your grifters on a bank security camera in Loveland, Colorado," Sean said.

"Is that all?"

"They set up an account using an Estes Park address." Sean handed Mr. Wishes a piece of note paper. "We took a look. They're still there."

"Very good. Your payment will reach you in the usual way."

"You don't want us to handle this?"

Mr. Wishes shook his head. "This is an in-house job."

# 15

Four days later, on the night of a new moon, long after Randy and Jodi had gone to bed, Randy heard a beeping in his earpiece. His eyes snapped open. The silent front-door alarm. He clapped his hand over Jodi's mouth and put his lips to her ear. "Front door."

She nodded her head, rolled off her side of the bed, and picked up her SIG Sauer. Randy did the same. He moved to the bedroom door, stood beside it, and listened. Jodi, dressed in a T-shirt and sleep shorts, crept into the bathroom, closed the door to a crack, went to the window, and raised it very slowly. She unhooked the window screen and let it fall. It landed in the bushes. She stuck her head out. The only light came from the streetlights in the parking lot. She peered at the deck. No one was standing there, but the patio door looked like it was open. She snuck back through the bathroom and knelt behind the doorjamb on the lock side. She pulled the door open a few inches. She could see Randy at the bedroom door.

Randy crouched there in his pajama pants, watching the doorknob. He could hear people moving quietly around the living room. When the doorknob started to turn, he fired twice through the wall beside the doorjamb. Someone howled and fell. Randy dropped to the floor. Rapid gunfire splintered the door and wall above him. He waited, peeking under the door as best he could. When the shooting stopped, he could feel footfalls approaching the door. He fired twice under the door. Someone shouted. He jumped to his feet and ran back to the bathroom. The bedroom door crashed open. Jodi emptied her clip into the opening while Randy scrambled behind her.

A smoke grenade rolled into the bedroom. Randy fired into the smoke. Jodi scurried across the bathroom, climbed out the window, and dropped into the bushes below, scraping her legs on some branches. Then she ran across the parking lot to their backup car, a used Chevy, reached under the bumper for the key fob, and climbed into the driver's seat.

When Randy saw her open the car door, he dropped out of the bathroom window, rolled, and got up and ran for the car. A man appeared in the window, firing a rifle. Slugs stitched across the asphalt. A ricochet caught Randy in the back as he reached the passenger's side door. He rolled into the car. "Drive," he yelled.

Jodi sped out of the parking lot with the headlights off, flipped them on when she got to the highway, and turned left to head down the mountain toward Denver.

"How bad?"

"Not sure. Not bleeding too much. No exit wound. Didn't get my lungs. Doesn't hurt too much. Keep driving."

Randy reached into the glove box and got out a burner phone. "Billy?"

"Traveling Man. It's a little late for you. What do you need?"

"Medical attention for a gunshot wound."

"How soon?"

"Not an emergency yet."

"Where are you?"

"Between Estes Park and Denver."

"This number good?"

"Yes."

"I'll call you back." Billy ended the call.

Jodi glanced at him. "Do I need to pull over?"

"We need to get away from that house."

"How many were they?"

"I don't know, but we killed at least two."

"This wasn't Kennedy."

"No, definitely not. Probably the Orange Hill Cartel."

"They stay pissed off a long time."

"Some of the gems were probably theirs."

"Well, they got them back."

"If they find them."

They drove down a switchback and over a small rise. Then the road started following a creek. There were no headlights behind them.

"I'm pulling over." Jodi pulled off the road by some picnic tables. "You sit there." She opened the trunk and dug around in their Go-bag for their first aid kit. Then she trotted around to the passenger's side and opened the car door. "Lean forward."

Randy put his arms on the dashboard. A truck zoomed by, its headlights slicing across them, but it didn't slow down.

Jodi examined his wound. "This is fucked up, baby. Billy better come through." She poured clotting powder on the entrance wound, lay a wad of gauze on it, and taped the gauze to his back. "That's the best I can do."

"You need to put clothes on."

She went back to the trunk, pulled on a pair of jeans and a cardigan sweater, found a pair of sneakers, and brought a flannel shirt to Randy. He pulled it on. "Let's get out of here."

They continued down the mountain, driving the speed limit, keeping on the lookout for vehicles acting suspiciously.

A few minutes later, Billy called back. "I got a paramedic for you. Military experience. She's expecting you. I'll text you her address."

"Thanks."

Jodi handed her phone to Randy. "Put the address in the map app and set a course."

Jodi followed the voice commands to a log cabin on a gravel road. As she pulled up in the front yard, a woman dressed in jeans and wearing a Kevlar vest over her T-shirt came out on the porch in the dark, cradling a shotgun. "Who are you?"

Jodi lowered her window. "Billy sent us."

"Park in the back."

Jodi drove around the side yard to the back of the house. The outside lights came on, and the paramedic came out the back door without her Kevlar vest. She was a tall, light-skinned Black woman whose hair was braided down her back. She came down the steps to the passenger's side of the car and opened the door.

"Thanks for seeing us," Jodi said.

The paramedic nodded and then turned to Randy. "Where were you shot?"

"In the upper back."

"Can you walk?"

"Yes."

"Let's go."

She helped him out of the car and up the steps into the kitchen, Jodi following close behind. "On the table."

The kitchen table was covered in a white sheet, a pillow at one end. A medical bag sat on a kitchen chair close at hand. Randy pulled off his flannel shirt and climbed onto the table.

The paramedic looked him over. "No shoes and wearing your jammies. Must have been in a hurry."

"Still are," Jodi replied.

The paramedic peeled off the tape and removed the gauze from the wound. "What was it?"

"Rifle slug," Randy said.

"Didn't go in far, looks like." She studied the wound. "I can't put you under, but I can give you a local and dig it out. You should really go to the hospital."

"If we could do that, we wouldn't be here."

She nodded, took two pill bottles out of her medical bag, and handed Randy four pills, two from each bottle.

"What are they?" Randy asked.

"Antibiotics and oxycodone. Won't knock you out, but ought to make things easier." She turned to Jodi. "Get him a glass of water."

Randy took the pills. The paramedic washed her hands and put on medical gloves. Then she took a syringe from its packaging, loaded it from a small bottle of lidocaine, and injected several places around the wound.

"You do much of this work?" Jodi asked.

"Not much anymore. Just for special friends."

"Like Billy?"

"Yeah."

"How long have you known him?"

"That's not something to get into. I get the idea that he's good at making friends with various skill sets. Let's leave it at that." She pointed to a bag containing medical gloves. "Put some gloves on." Then she turned to Randy. "You should be numb now."

She took a scalpel and made a small incision at each end of the wound to widen the hole. The she inserted a thin clamp and opened it to stretch the hole. "How much does this hurt?"

"Not too much."

She put the syringe into the wound and added more numbing agent. "That should help in a bit. I've got to feel for the bullet now. If it's in pieces, someone else—someone with an x-ray—will have to finish the job."

She inserted another clamp into the hole and felt carefully for the bullet. Blood began to ooze from the wound. Randy grunted and gripped the sides of the table.

"I've got something." She closed the clamp and backed it slowly out of the wound. The blood ran more freely. She looked at the mashed bullet. "Ricochet. Looks like the whole thing." She dropped it into Jodi's hand.

"I hope you're right," Randy said.

The paramedic mopped up the blood. "Hold the gauze down," she said to Jodi.

While Jodi applied pressure, the paramedic opened a suture kit. "Okay," she said.

Jodi removed the gauze, and the paramedic sutured the wound closed. Then she applied two Steri-Strips, some gauze, and tape.

She looked at Randy. "How do you feel?"

"Better than I should."

"It's going to hurt like hell in a few hours. I can give you enough oxy to carry you through tomorrow, but that's all."

"Appreciate it."

She turned to Jodi. "You need to get an x-ray to be sure all the metal is out of there and to evaluate if something more should be done."

"Okay."

"Help me up," Randy said. "We need to get going."

The paramedic helped him sit up. "Don't stand if you're dizzy."

"I'm okay."

Jodi helped Randy put on his shirt. Then she and the paramedic helped him down from the table and out to the car, where he lay down in the back seat.

"You were never here," the paramedic said.

"Already forgot the way," Jodi replied. She opened the trunk, dug around in a duffel bag, and found a manila envelope of cash. She counted out $2,000 in hundreds and handed it to the paramedic.

"Thanks for your help."

The paramedic nodded.

Jodi put the envelope back into the duffel before she shut the trunk and climbed into the driver's seat. She drove back around the cabin to the gravel road. "How're you doing back there?"

"I'm okay. Groggy."

"I'll try to avoid the bumps." She drove slowly down the gravel until she reached the county road and turned toward Denver.

"Our cover is blown," she said.

"Yep. It's the only way they could have found us."

"What do you want to do?"

"Stop at an interstate motel and stay overnight. Then run for Salt Lake City. IDs will hold up that long."

"Use the emergency IDs from the safe deposit box in Salt Lake City?"

"We've got no choice."

"Are you sure those IDs are still good?"

"That forger died of a heart attack. No one can get to him. And his work was top drawer."

"Okay." She merged onto the busy interstate behind a semitruck. "At least we've still got the money."

"Yeah. We won't be living in style, but we'll be living. And we'll be able to stay lost long enough to escape from the FBI and the Orange Hill Cartel."


MR. WISHES ROLLED over in bed and picked up his business phone from the night table. "Speak."

"The good news is we got the gems and the bonds."

"And the bad news?"

"They shot three of ours and got away."

Mr. Wishes sat up and turned on the bedside lamp. "But you put a tracker on their car."

"They had a second car. If they had have gone for the one we knew about, they'd be dead."

"Clean up the mess and bring me the gems and the bonds." Mr. Wishes ended the call. Those fucking grifters. His guys had underestimated them again. He set his phone down. Their default preparation was at such a high level that nothing could be left to chance if he was going to catch them. Should have let Sean and Phyllis have them. He turned off the light and lay down. Kennedy sure caught a break. The bonds and everything except the diamonds were his. Now he'd get them back.

The next morning, while he was sitting at the back table of a café he frequented, drinking coffee and reading the newspaper on his smartphone, Sean and Phyllis came through the front door. A waitress started toward them with two menus. "It's okay, Charlene," Mr. Wishes said. "They're with me."

Sean and Phyllis walked back to Mr. Wishes' table. "Have a seat," he said.

They sat cattycorner to Mr. Wishes so that they could see who was coming in the front door. "What can we do for you?" Sean said.

"I need for you to hunt down the grifters."

"The same ones?" Phyllis asked.

He nodded.

"How many did you send?" Sean asked.

"Six."

"How many came back?"

"Three. You got your work cut out for you."

"Where were they last seen?"

"At that condo in Estes Park."

"Do you need them alive?" Phyllis asked.

"I need them dead," Mr. Wishes replied.

Sean nodded at Phyllis. They stood up. "We'll be in touch."

FBI AGENT JAMES POWERS stood in the lower parking lot behind the condo Randy and Jodi had rented, talking with the sheriff's chief deputy. Yellow police tape and sheriff's department vehicles cordoned off the condo and a large section on the parking lot. Most of the windows of the condo had been shot out, and numbered markers indicated where bullets had stopped on the pavement.

"Early this morning?" Powers asked.

"Looks like a drug crew turf war," the deputy said. "Shot this place up like it was Bagdad."

"But no bodies?"

"No bodies. Three blood slicks. Looks like three guys were dragged off."

"And the folks who were renting the condo?"

"Their car is up top. No damage. No fingerprints. Turns out it was stolen."

"Stolen? And no fingerprints? None at all?"

"Not a one. What's your interest anyway?"

"Violent crime taskforce. This is the kind of thing that gets the governor's attention. Bad for tourism."

"Yep."

"Thanks for your cooperation."

Powers went back to his Ford Explorer and called Agent Cooper.

"Did you get a match with the Loveland bank customers?"

"Yes," Powers replied.

"Using an Airbnb as a banking address. Had to be the Suttons. So now we have their alias."

"If they're not dead."

"They're not dead. If they were, we'd have the bodies. Who do the sheriffs think was after them?"

"Drug crew."

"It wasn't a drug crew."

"No, sir, but they were some heavy hitters."

"Keep after them. The window is going to close on this current alias."

"If they stayed in a motel, we'll find them."


KENNEDY WAS AT HIS OFFICES, reading through the inventory of a high-end gem broker in Antwerp, when his burner phone rang. Mr. Wishes. What could he want?

"Hello."

"Hello, Kennedy. How are you?"

"I'm still working on getting your money together. Almost have it. Just need a few more days—maybe a week."

"I've got some good news for you."

"Good news?"

"We retrieved the gems and the bonds. One of my guys will be bringing them to you."

"The gems? So you got your diamonds back?"

"Exactly."

"And I get my gems and my bonds?"

"You're on our team, Jackson. We play fair with everyone on our team."

"What about my cash?"

"Didn't get the cash. And I wouldn't count on getting it back now."

"But we're square?"

"Yes. It's business as usual. We'll be in touch when we need you." Mr. Wishes ended the call.

Kennedy swiveled his chair and looked out the window into the back parking lot. He'd collected most of the cash he needed to pay the Orange Hill Cartel from the Cayman account. It was sitting in the safe. But now he didn't need to pay them. And Brenda didn't know he didn't need to pay them. Plus he'd gotten the gems and the bearer bonds back. And she didn't know about that, either. It was like Christmas and winning the lottery. It was almost as if the grifters had done him a favor, except for the cash. He could hide away the gems, the bonds, and the Cayman money. Keep Brenda from finding out about them. Then he wouldn't have to share them in the divorce settlement. He'd tried to be fair with her, but she just wasn't willing to meet him halfway. Always bitching, always demanding. What he needed now was a good divorce lawyer.

Six days later, Sean and Phyllis were sitting with Mr. Wishes in his booth at the Atlas Tavern.

"So you've got nothing?"

"We traced them to a Quality Inn outside Denver," Sean said. "We got their car's make, model, license plate number. Made no difference. Found the car at a truck stop in Utah. Never saw another surveillance image of either of them."

"We'll keep looking," Phyllis said, "but I don't think we're going to find them. Not right now, anyway."

Mr. Wishes sipped his coffee. "No, stop wasting your time. They'll turn up eventually. We'll just have to be patient. When we find their trail, I'll be back in touch."

"Probably for the best," Sean said.

.    .    .

AGENT POWERS SAT in Agent Cooper's office. Cooper closed his laptop computer and looked up. "What have you got for me?"

"The Suttons weren't killed in Estes Park. We had a solid sighting outside Denver. Circumstantial evidence they went to Salt Lake City, but nothing actionable."

"Meaning?"

"We're working in a circle out from Salt Lake, but we haven't found anything yet."

"The trail is completely cold?"

"I wish I had a lead for you, boss."

"Not your fault, James. Smith screwed this up to begin with. If you had been running that sting, I'm sure we'd have them in custody."

"How do you want to proceed, sir?"

"There're too many ongoing investigations that need our attention. We're going to have to put the Suttons on the back burner."

"Yes, sir."


A WEEK LATER, Chrissie was walking between classes on campus when she heard her work phone ringing in her backpack. She swung her pack off her shoulder and pulled the phone from the outer pocket. She looked at the screen. It was Ms. Gleason.

"Hello?"

"Hello, Chrissie. Have you got a minute?"

"Sure." Chrissie stepped off the sidewalk to get out of the way of the other students hurrying to class.

"You've seen the election results?"

"Yes."

"Lucky the video didn't show your face."

"You've seen the video?"

"Of course."

"That's awkward."

"Not as much as it could be. The new prosecuting attorney hasn't got a clue as to what's going on. If you're still interested in coming back, we'd love to have you."

"Same rate?"

"Same rate."

"Do I get my old clients back?"

"Most of them."

Chrissie smiled. "When do I start?"

THE NEXT MORNING, at a cabin near Mount Hood, Oregon, Randy turned off the TV and came out onto the porch with two cups of coffee. "Incredible view, huh?"

The sun was just breaking over the mountains to the east, the clouds glowing red in the first light. Randy handed Jodi a cup of coffee and sat down on the front porch glider next to her. He was wearing a jacket over his pajamas, and she was wearing a thick robe. "News roundup showed Little Pap coming out of the courthouse. Indicted for conspiracy."

Jodi sipped her coffee, set the cup down on the end table, and pulled her fuzzy robe tight around her body. She took Randy's hand in hers and squeezed. "Do you think we might have overstepped by sending evidence to the newspaper?"

"Little Pap could have played fair. Could have gotten paid. Instead he chose to try to screw us."

"So we settled up with Little Pap and Brighton. It's been a crazy few months. I'm glad they're over."

"Me, too," Randy replied. "And I'm glad we're already geared up. I don't even want to contact Billy for a while."

"How much trouble do you think Kennedy is in?"

"That depends on whether he got the gems and the bonds back. Not that I care. He deserves all the trouble he gets."

"And Chrissie?"

He shrugged. "You warned her. She'll have to figure it out herself."

"She didn't make any money."

"She wanted to be a player. Planned to sell us out every chance she got. I know she's just a kid, but whatever happened to her is on her."

Jodi lifted his hand and kissed it. "It's always us."

"Us against the world." Randy pointed with his free hand. A large bird floated high over the valley in the distance looking for prey. "What kind of bird is that?"

"Hawk, eagle, I don't know. It's pretty big."

Randy kissed her neck. "Three more days here. Then we head to our next safehouse."

"What do you want to do to pass the time?"

He hugged her close. "Let's fire up the hot tub."

# FINALLY

Thanks for reading *Grifters' Hopscotch*. If you enjoyed it, please post a short review on a review site of your choice. A few words will do. Honest reviews are the number one way I attract new readers. Thanks so much.

I'd love to hear from you. You can reach me at my website: https://michaelpking.org

**The KD Thorne Thrillers**

*The Hunt for the Hijacked Nerve Agent*

*Murder at Mercy Creek*

*The Hunt for the Ransomware Hackers*

**The Travelers**

*The Double Cross: A Travelers Prequel*

*The Traveling Man: Book One*

*The Computer Heist: Book Two*

*The Blackmail Photos: Book Three*

*The Freeport Robbery: Book Four*

*The Kidnap Victim: Book Five*

*The Murder Run: Book Six*

*The Casino Switcheroo: Book Seven*

*Thicker Than Thieves: Book Eight*

*The Dark Web Scam: Book Nine*

*Grifters' Hopscotch: Book Ten*